LEFT-HANDED DEATH

RICHARD HULL

AGORA BOOKS

ABOUT THE AUTHOR

Richard Hull was born Richard Henry Sampson in London on 6 September 1896 to Nina Hull and SA Sampson, and attended Rugby School, Warwickshire. When the First World War broke out, his uncle helped him secure a commission in the Queen Victoria's Rifles. At the end of the war, after three years in France, he returned to England and worked as an accountant.

His first book, *The Murder of My Aunt*, written under the pseudonym Richard Hull, was published in 1934. The novel, set in Dysserth, Welshpool, is known for its humour, narrative charm, and unexpected twists. Hull moved to writing full-time in 1934 and wrote a further fourteen novels over the span of his career.

During the Second World War, he became an auditor with the Admiralty in London — a position he retained for eighteen years until he retired in 1958. While he stopped writing detective fiction after 1953, Hull continued to take an interest in the affairs of the Detection Club, assisting Agatha Christie with her duties as President. He died in 1973.

ALSO BY RICHARD HULL

The Murder of My Aunt
Keep It Quiet
Murder Isn't Easy
The Ghost It Was
The Murderers of Monty
Excellent Intentions
And Death Came Too
My Own Murderer
The Unfortunate Murderer
Left Handed Death
Last First
Until She Was Dead
A Matter of Nerves
Invitation to an Inquest
The Martineau Murders

LEFT-HANDED DEATH

RICHARD HULL

This edition published in 2019 by Agora Books

Agora Books is a division of Peters Fraser + Dunlop Ltd

First published in Great Britain in 1946 by The Collins Crime Club

55 New Oxford Street, London WC1A 1BS

Copyright © Richard Hull, 1946

All rights reserved

You may not copy, distribute, transmit, reproduce or otherwise make available this publication (or any part of it) in any form, or by any means (including without limitation electronic, digital, optical, mechanical, photocopying, printing, recording or otherwise), without the prior written permission of the publisher. Any person who does any unauthorised act in relation to this publication may be liable to criminal prosecution and civil claims for damages.

PART I

"I tell it you for the strange coolness which the young fellow...expressed as he was writing his confession. 'I murd—' he stopped and asked, 'How do you spell murdered?'"

— HORACE WALPOLE. *LETTER* 863.

Arthur Shergold walked into his office on the first floor and shut the door behind him with exaggerated care. Then he went across to the window and closed that too, despite the hottest April sun that he could remember. There was a look of pleasure in his eyes as he noiselessly shut out the last breath of air.

It was gone, however, as he turned round to face young Guy Reeves who was sitting negligently in the chair by a writing desk, with one leg thrown over the arm. There was a sleepy far away expression on the young man's face and he appeared to be pleased with himself.

Shergold leant over him and peered closely into the half-shut black eyes. In a half whisper he asked a question that was almost a statement. "So you have done it?"

For a moment there was silence while Reeves looked a little petulantly at the window. "Isn't it rather hot?" he suggested.

Shergold's thin lips met determinedly above his heavy chin but he did not try to avoid the evasion. "We haven't got the fire alight. And anyhow you can't be too careful when you're talking about such things as — such things as we are going to talk about." He paused and then went on. "We are going to talk about it, you know."

But Reeves hardly seemed to be listening. His eyelids kept on half-closing and concealing his big dark eyes. His left arm was stretched out on the desk showing that three fingers of it had gone, leaving nothing beyond the knuckles while as well the thumb and the first finger still remained. He was in a queer way rather proud of that hand; it was both his proof that he had fought — in Tunis as it happened — and his means of getting his own way by playing on this disability. It was almost more a convenience to him than a handicap and he had no intention of concealing it. He looked down on it now as he spoke. "We may talk — since you insist. But I don't see why I should be stifled while I do it."

"Oh! Security!" Shergold tried to laugh it off, but there was a hint of determination behind his apparently careless tone.

"Security be blowed. It nearly always was nonsense. You'll be telling me next that Cynthia Trent is listening at the key-hole."

"The key—" Shergold moved rapidly to the door and flung it open. The few yards of passage that led to the top of the staircase were empty nor was there anyone, a quick glance told him, in Reeves room or in the room next door, once (when such things had been necessary) a fire-watchers' room and still fitted up though rather simply as a bedroom. There was another door at the top of the stairs which could be used to shut off the three rooms from the rest of the offices of the Shergold Engineering Company Ltd and make of them almost a self-contained flat. With a gesture of impatience, as if he was cross with himself for not having thought of it before, the founder and chairman of the Company shut the outer door and locked it. Again he shut the office door with unnecessary care. "Better be safe than sorry," he remarked with a feeble giggle that seemed out of character with his determined appearance.

The giggle was apparently the last straw. Reeves got up very slowly and drew himself up to his full six foot two. He was an inch or two taller than Shergold and he made what use he could of that. "Are you having the impertinence," he asked, "to take my remarks about Cynthia seriously? To suggest that she could really listen at a key-hole?"

"Hullo! This is a new — no, of course I am not. Last person in the world. But there's no point in running risks. You've avoided them so far, haven't you?"

"Of course I have. What do you take me for? A blithering idiot?" Reeves seemed mollified and once more he sank back into the revolving writing chair and yawned. Shergold looked at him keenly and wiped a bead of sweat from his forehead. "Perhaps it is a bit hot," he admitted grudgingly and with a swift change of idea he flung open the two windows top and bottom. "Have it just as you like," he said. "Oh, never mind if the papers do blow about."

"But I do mind. I simply cannot be bothered to go on picking them up all the time. Those are Foster's last figures that nearly went out of the window then. Can't you keep a sense of proportion? Shut 'em all if you like."

"Thanks. Really, I think it is best. You can never be sure of April. Not even in 1945. And we must not lose anything of Foster's. Not now."

"No, certainly not now." There was a pause, and then, almost irrelevantly he went on, "Was there anything of interest in those figures?"

"Not really. Further demands that we repay money to the Government. With every contract finished and closed down and no sign of any new ones coming! How he hopes we can refund money, I've no idea."

"Why haven't we got any more contracts?"

"I don't know. Foster's fault, I think. All this prying into our accounts. He — or rather the Government — is entitled to, I suppose — in fact, I know they are, or I wouldn't have let him — but all the same, it's more than a darned nuisance and I think he's put the Ministry against us. These components for instance." He picked up a steel tube with a heavy end to it most delicately machined. "I hoped we were going to get a decent contract for them which would have kept us going nicely. But apparently there's nothing doing. So I repeat, I'm almost sure that he has put the Ministry against us."

"Well, he won't do that anymore."

* * *

THERE WERE many deficiencies in Barry Foster's work for the Ministry who employed him, but "putting the Ministry against us" could hardly be called one. He was far too idle and lazy to do anything of the sort and his principal object, especially during the latter part of the five years that he had worked for them, had been to get through his duties easily and without argument or fuss. His method was a simple one. He was quite prepared to give to the Companies that he visited every point that they asked for, provided that it was not too directly opposed to his written instructions and provided also that it was impossible to conceal that fact from his department. When that point had been reached, he used to put on what he hoped was an ingratiating smile — it was in fact rather an oleaginous leer — and murmur that he was awfully sorry. "I really can't do that, you know. You can probably guess what my employers are. Awfully nice chaps really, and quite sensible too, but they have principles unfortunately, and they will go and stick to them. Very obstinate at times, I fear. It's no good my putting that in. I should only get it referred back to me and I should not be able to explain it away."

"You have to explain what you have done and why?" was the

question that generally came next and Foster used to answer it with a further smile and a slightly self-depreciatory gesture of the left hand. "Oh, yes! I'm not allowed to take responsibility. No one is in a Government Department; you know I have to be checked like the rest." Perhaps more companies than he would have liked to have thought considered that, though the Ministry who employed him were often very tiresome, they were right in not giving Mr Barry Foster too free a hand. Still as Foster used to say when he saw fit to bore his friends with the subject, it did not matter what contractors thought of him provided they agreed to those things that his department really insisted upon. "I give them all the doubtful points I can, my dear chap. Whether it cost the taxpayer more or less does not seem to me to matter one hoot. On the whole, I do not think that it does, and, in any case, those sort of things can be safely left to the Excess Profits Tax. It gives me a little peace and quiet — from both sides of the argument — and really, you know, I feel entitled to some peace."

The Shergold Engineering Company however had long given him a "pain in the neck." So far as he could see there was nothing wrong with it. Shergold always had his figures ready, they always looked convincing and there was always an explanation for everything. He did not like Shergold himself, but they gave you a good lunch and there was always that Miss Trent to look at. How they got her deferred from various "call-ups" he had no idea but there she was, and she produced figures about materials — those as to labour Shergold passed on to her — and she did calculations on a machine gladly and they were right, which Foster was prepared laughingly to admit "is more than you can say for mine." Then he would look serious and add "unless of course I really give my mind to it." He hoped to produce an impression of carefully concealed but invariable competence modestly veiled by a jesting pretence of being something of an amateur at a matter which was really rather beneath his dignity. It was tiresome though when someone, particularly the department, failed to penetrate the veil. For his desire for peace and quiet never went so far as to admit that he could be wrong.

In the matter of the Shergold Engineering Company, the department were being peculiarly difficult. They kept on pointing out the blunt fact remained that the work that they did was more than a little bit more expensive than it ought to be and there did not seem to be any particular reason why it should be. Positively the department insisted on Mr Foster finding out why.

"Though how they think I am going to do it," he complained to one of his colleagues, "I have no idea. There are the facts and for the life of me I cannot see what else I can do."

"What is said to be expensive?"

"I simply do not know. They will not trust me by showing me anyone else's costs, but I gather the labour's too high." The discussion had drifted off on to professional points of what was charged direct and what indirect and ended up with Foster's moan "That he was not an engineer — thank goodness — and he did not see how he was expected to carry out technical costing."

"You could get technical help."

"Yes, I know; and at the end they would tell me that it ought to cost so much and it may be true but that will not alter the fact that it has in fact cost half as much again. So we should not have advanced much."

His colleague had sighed and gone on with the work he was doing. Foster's obstinacy was well known. The only thing that was doubtful was whether it arose from conviction or from idleness. It took some while to see through Barry Foster's façade.

One who had seen through it from the start was Cynthia

Trent. She did not like the way he looked at her for one thing, but she was not going to give that as a reason. In fact it was a trouble that had arisen more than once since she had joined the Shergold Engineering Company and she was perfectly capable of dealing with it. Moreover she had always intended to stay with the company at any rate until the war was over and young Mr Reeves was back — and now that he was back, she still thought that he wanted some looking after. She had come just before he had been called up and on rather slight acquaintance and inadequate knowledge, had decided that his interests would need someone to mind them while he was away and that, though no one had asked her to do so, she would do just that. An absentee director with a minority holding was in a poor position, she thought, when the senior director was such a man as Shergold, whom she characterised as a shifty sort of person. Moreover Reeves, she imagined correctly, must have bought his shares and the job with them and probably paid too high a price. If too, as she believed was so, he was all too ignorant of what he should know as to engineering, he would be helpless in Shergold's grip, if Shergold so chose. She had even tried to point it out to Reeves when he came back invalided out of the Army. "You ought to get down to it. Even to understand the figures I produce would be something, but above all you ought to know how all these things are made and be able to make them yourself."

"I don't know. I don't think I should be very good at all that. Besides there are many things to do beside the technical details. There are the people in the works to look after and manage."

"You cannot do that in exactly the way you have been used to in the Army, you know."

"Perhaps not. Rather a pity, I think. All the same I am sure I can manage them a bit." It was quite clear from the way he said it, that he meant more than "a bit." *It's no good trying to argue with him when he's in that mood,* Cynthia had thought to herself and she had tried a different line. "I know you are very good with them," she had gone on out loud and perhaps less truthfully, "but it leaves too much to Mr Shergold if you stick to that side only."

"Too much what?"

"Oh, too much — well, control."

At that Reeves had rather snapped at her. "If it comes to a question of control, I think I can — shall we say? — hold my own."

"Oh, yes." With that Cynthia had had to let it drop, but she sighed all the same. She did not think it was true. Meanwhile all such matters as dealing with Barry Foster remained where they had been when Guy Reeves was in North Africa or in hospital in England recovering from the loss of those three fingers — that is to say Shergold dealt with everything that she did not. The way in which he kept all labour records in his hands was enough, she felt, to have made Reeves think. She would remember his first discussion on the subject with Foster, and she felt that he too ought to have thought more carefully about the subject.

"What sort of a system have you got?" Foster had asked. "A pretty good one?"

"I think so. I attend to it myself very largely," Shergold had told him. It passed through Cynthia's brain that from the point of view of the Ministry that was a doubtful advantage and that they might well prefer a division of responsibility as a method of preventing fraud, but Foster seemed to swallow it all easily and so she supposed had not got to worry. "Yes, I make up the wages book myself. See that it agrees in detail with the cost records and give Miss Trent the figures that she wants. The wages cheque and the cash pass through my hands — I even make up the pay packets sometimes. Finally, so that there should be no nonsense, I even see to the insurance cards."

"Really?" Even Foster looked surprised. "All that? The pay

packets too? Such dirty things coins. Besides, can you really give the time? You seem to me to have lots to do here."

"It's quite simple. I do it on fire-watching nights. It helps to pass the time. At least that is what I give out in the works and to some extent it's true, but of course it does give me an insight into that side. I have heard too many stories of people being robbed that way not to keep an eye on it."

"Good," Foster had yawned. "I shall not then have to worry you very much on that side. Perhaps just an occasional check on it and an occasional look at the insurance cards."

"Certainly." Shergold made no difficulty about that. Indeed he had clearly no need to do so, for it was quite clear to any observer that the check, if it ever occurred, would be very occasional and would be very unlikely to bring anything of interest to light.

In fact it might never have occurred at all if, as Foster put it, "some busybody had not started comparing costs. Probably not fair comparisons either." "You know," he was in the habit of saying, "you cannot — you simply can*not* (only my department will not recognise it), get a fair comparison these days. All sorts of different circumstances come into play — some people are doing work they are laid out to do, others are helping by doing something new to them and I do not see why they should be penalised for what are often very fine efforts. Free issues of materials complicates the thing too. Oh, no, it's absurd. But they think some good comes of it. If they would only believe what one has told them time after time and let one get on with it. But —" With a gesture he would indicate how much more he was a man of the world than was the Government Department that employed him. "Civil servants," he would mutter in a tone which implied that he had said something.

As to the refunds of which Shergold spoke so acidly, that bitterness of the tone would have surprised Foster not a little. Few and far between, he would have said they were and only when they really failed completely to justify the price quoted, had he insisted. It was worse than unpleasant to insist; it was a nuisance and involved hours of arguments that seemed to him utterly tedious. As to "putting the Ministry against us," in a way, but only in a literal way, that was wholly untrue. The Ministry's files were full of his angry expostulations (for he reserved such tact as he had for contractors and did not waste it on his own department) justifying the figures that he had submitted even if they could be proved to be wrong. "Mr Foster," his tired senior had once said, "I do not admire your habit of saying that two and two are five, but that is a minor matter compared with the additional habit that when you do so inadvertently, you positively stick to it, and I actively and violently hate your masterly justification of such statements."

"But I have never said that two and two were five. Now be fair. Where have I said such a thing? Show it to me. Just show it."

"Well, perhaps not literally."

"There you are then. Really—" Then with an obvious effort to regain his composure, he had, as it were, publicly forgiven his chief for the gross slander on his professional abilities. Mr Pennington, the luckless holder of that position, put out his hand for another of Mr Foster's files. It would be easy to prove his point but was it after all worthwhile? His hand was withdrawn.

Nevertheless, in another way, Foster had put the Ministry against the Shergold Engineering Company, and for that matter against many of the other firms that he visited. They had all become bones of contention of which too much had been heard (if a bone of contention can be heard), and it would be pleasant to hear no more of them. With the need for munitions becoming less, contracts need not be given to everyone and the costs of the Shergold Engineering Company were undoubtedly high. A quiet hint from one part of the Ministry to another would not be amiss and would not be neglected.

***

But whether Foster had or had not thus adversely affected the fortunes of the Shergold Engineering Company, Reeves was clear as to one thing. He would not do so again.

It was a queer scene that was taking place on that Wednesday of April 18th. The sunlight poured in on to the desk and chair where Reeves sat leaning right back in it lazily, as if he had not a care in the world. Of the two it was the older man who was showing signs, if there were any, of nerves; though even the closest observer could have told of them only by the concentration of his attention on Reeves. His eyes never seemed to leave the younger man for a second. Yet with all the riveting of his glance, the younger man hardly seemed to notice it, except that he did not seem anxious to talk. He had sunk back into almost a trance and again he yawned but he did not seem inclined to speak.

"No more," Shergold prompted, but Reeves said nothing and Shergold had to go on. "Did you do it as—" Reeves stirred and Shergold changed the form of the question hurriedly. "Where did you do it?" he corrected. "Were you right about where he lived? It was clever of you to have found that out."

"Yes," Reeves accepted the word of praise without comment, "though you gave me a hint. But I say, Arthur, how does he afford it? It was quite a nice little flat, up Maida Vale way. It cannot have been cheap, and I have always heard that Government salaries—"

"I thought I told you how he afforded it."

"I know what you said as far as we are concerned. It was a further proof of what I always thought, that he was a dirty dog. But it was not much of a sum."

"I do not suppose we were the only ones."

"That would surprise me a little. It's a risky game to try on too many people and it would only require that he should find one person who was overly scrupulous, and the game would be up. How did he open up the subject to you?"

Shergold seemed not to be ready with an answer or not to like the subject. "Oh! I hardly know," he began hesitatingly. "A hint or two. Did he mention the cost of the flat? Perhaps that was where I got hold of where it was. I forget. Anyhow—"

"Anyhow you saw what he was getting at and met him half-way, I suppose?"

"Something like that. But that is not what I am interested in." Shergold's eyes seemed to bore into Reeves' brain. "That is not the point. Leave that out."

"Quite." Reeves seemed to sink back again into a coma and once more Shergold had to prompt him. "Let me remind you again. When you came back from Tunis and got down to work here, you found that the Company on which your livelihood depended was not as prosperous as you thought. It had not made very much out of Government contracts and moreover it had none left to carry out. You questioned your fellow director who had been in charge while you had been away and very reluctantly—" Reeves stirred uneasily and Shergold modified his statement. "Well, reluctantly then, he told you that he put it down to Foster's interference, directly by — what we have just discussed, but I would forget that — forget that entirely," he repeated emphatically, almost as if it were a command.

"All right. But I do not see why—"

"Much better to leave it out. This cutting down of our prices and the trouble he has got us into are quite enough."

"Besides there is — but perhaps better not mention…" Reeves seemed to be dozing off.

"I do not know what you have in mind," Shergold's glance seemed to be uneasy as if he were wondering whether to probe the matter further, but finally he apparently decided to let it rest. "Stick to what we know already. Prices. Trouble. Absence of contracts." He leant forward and emphasised the three points.

"Quite." Reeves sat up suddenly and begun talking quite briskly. "So I decided to have it out with him and if necessary, to do what we had agreed."

"No," Shergold was quite firm about it. "What you thought right. I never had the courage. All these years I was prepared to put up with it. But when a man of action such as you came back…"

"Right again. It took somebody like me." Reeves was suddenly buoyant now. He seemed to have forgotten Shergold entirely and the words came rolling out. "I repeat. So I decided to have it out with him — I wish you would not interrupt — and do what I thought right. It was a neat discovery to find out that he was in the habit of doing what he called work in his own flat instead of going back to his office. I strongly suspect that it gave him plenty of excuses to be absent when he wanted to be."

"He used to say that his office was too full and too noisy for anyone to work there."

"Yes, yes, I know. So the only difficulty to get over was to find an excuse for going there, instead of bringing him here. I thought I got round that admirably." Reeves played idly with the rejected component lying on the desk and waited for the obvious question.

Nor did he have to wait long. It came quite quickly.

"How did you do that?"

"I started by asking him out to lunch. He would always fall for that — especially when I suggested that it must be a very good lunch, because I understood from you that he had done so very much during the war to get things settled and I wanted to say, 'thank you.' The vanity of that man! He must have known that he had not only done nothing for us but had actually ruined us. However he fell for it. It must be frightful to be as vain as that."

"I see what you mean. It's all right to have a proper respect for yourself when you have something to be proud of — but otherwise — sorry, I'm interrupting. Go on."

"Quite. Then I suggested that as papers were a nuisance to him, he should not bring them but should leave them at home. I would be quite willing to go back to his place afterwards. I pointed out that it was no distance to his flat from plenty of good restaurants. We could even get a bus if we could not get a taxi — and he fell for that too in the end. I think there was a moment when he hesitated, when he wondered whether he wanted me to see his flat. You know he liked to pretend he was a more important person in the Ministry than he was. I don't believe his room in the Ministry was as good as he would have liked it to be. An expert on the Civil Service can tell a man's salary from the pattern on the oil-cloth — if any."

"But the flat was sufficiently presentable."

"Exactly. In fact I think he decided in the end it was more than that. It would even do him credit. By the way, I quite forgot to tell you: He told me to tell you that if any telephone messages came here, you were to say that he was out for the minute but would be back — no, you told me he said that; I was forgetting. Anyhow were there any?"

"No. I wonder why he did that? Probably he was supposed to be here."

"To cover up the fact that he was doing nothing. It's more than likely that he claimed the fare to here. A mean cuss." Reeves suddenly grinned. "If he has claimed it, it will look rather odd on his travelling claim if he has written it up already. Anyhow…"

But Shergold seemed to be deliberating. His eyes wandered for a moment from Reeves' face. "I suppose he would not write it up in advance. But you were saying…" Once more he concentrated on the younger man.

"I gave him the dickens of a lunch. It cost—" He got out his pocket book. "That's odd," he said. "I thought I had used most of the money I had on me."

"You forget. I have just refunded you the fiver."

"Have you? I do not seem — but anyhow there it is. A fiver, was it? I suppose it cost me that. It certainly was a good lunch."

Shergold leant forward. "Tell me about it," he said. "It must have been rather an odd feeling considering what you had in mind."

But Reeves seemed strangely disinclined to talk. He looked vaguely at Shergold. "I hardly believe — Do you know I really am not sure whether I had any lunch at all? All I know is that I feel extraordinarily hungry, especially considering — Five pounds did you say I spent? It was not likely to have been in fact the exact figure, I suppose?"

"That was what I gave you." Shergold looked intently at him as if he was anxious to impress something on his mind. "You must get your details right. Remember you are going to repeat all this soon, and to a very critical audience. You would be angry if they caught you out in some detail."

Reeves sat up abruptly. "They will not be able to do that. Of course I shall have the whole thing consistent and accurate. 'Catching me out?'" He gave a suppressed snort of contempt for the idea.

"Very well then. That's why I want to go over it all with you."

"We went to the Café Royal." His head sank forward and then he sat up suddenly. "What nonsense! You're putting ideas into my head. We went to Oddenino's."

"Very well then. But get it right. Oddenino's."

"And you had for lunch?"

"How should I know?"

"Try to remember. You had a drink beforehand?"

"Perhaps. It is usual. And this time I was not to spoil the ship, you remember."

"A rum cocktail?"

"Yes, only they called it something different."

"They might. Anyhow that was what it was. And you liked it." There was no answer from Reeves, so Shergold went on. "You only had one."

"No, two. I always have two."

"Oh very well." For a moment the obstruction seemed to annoy Shergold but then he went on. "That was at the bar outside the dining room. Downstairs."

"Was it? You know best. I thought it was on the ground floor. And that then, we moved across. Are you sure it was not on the ground floor?"

"No, it would not be — though it could. You must be clear headed—"

Suddenly Reeves jumped up in anger. "Of course I am clear headed. What the hell do you mean by suggesting that I am not? If one is not clear about all the details that happened before… before one…before one did what I have done," (he threw out his chest as he spoke), "when would one be clear? For you to suggest that I do not know every detail, is…is…"

"All right, all right. I only want to be quite sure. Of course you have got the picture absolutely clear. I never knew anyone with so exact a mind. You're taking it simply marvellously. I know I should not be so calm about it, if I were you."

"But then you never would be. You would never have the guts."

Shergold swallowed the insult and went back to where they had been. "Two rum cocktails downstairs then. Costing?"

"I forget. One gives a note and perhaps they give you something back and you tell them to keep it. That must be why the cost was a round figure."

"Quite. And then you went in to lunch?"

"And then we went in to lunch. And we had some smoked salmon and a grilled sole and lamb chops with new potatoes cooked in butter and some mushrooms and it cost…oh, a devil of a lot."

"It would," said Shergold drily. "I like your joke. But rationing still being on…"

"Rationing. Yes, that's why I'm still feeling hungry. I say, Shergold, did I really have any lunch at all?"

"You would hardly stop short at cocktails, would you?"

"No, I suppose not."

"But you would not be able to have the lunch you wanted and have just described. That's the lunch of your dreams and likely to remain that for some time. You had in fact — Hors d'oeuvres?"

"Yes. At least I did. He had *pâté maison*. Very filling — I don't like the stuff and after all it's really nothing very much more than glorified potted meat. But he liked it and so he had lots of that. And then, something. Venison, I think. It usually is that. Or rather it usually is pigeon. But not today — I just simply cannot eat pigeon."

Once more Reeves' attention seemed to be wandering and Shergold had to bring him back to the point. "Venison, then, for both of you. And an ice. And to drink?"

"We had a bottle of claret."

Shergold looked a little doubtful. "I suppose you ought to know the vineyard. Perhaps even the year."

"Why on earth? In these days you take what they give you and try to look pleased. Damned extravagant of old Foster to want anything like that, even if…especially as…"

"I can imagine his asking for it. Do you remember when we were talking about this subject the other day, we thought we could imagine the scene?"

"Yes. I don't believe though we put in claret then. Stingy of you not to. Because I had to do it as we planned it. I think you might have allowed me fizz!"

"For a fiver! They probably had not got any anyhow. Did you look?"

"No."

"Very well then. Stick to claret — and remember exactly how it went."

The scene seemed to act itself in Reeves' imagination quite clearly. He could see himself sitting at the table with Barry Foster opposite to him. It was all he could do to keep his eyes off the accountant's thick throat. There was a roll of fat in the man's jowl that was fascinating. Moreover he had seldom seen a man whose head was so close to his shoulders. There was hardly any neck at all in one sense. Yet in another there was a great deal too much of it. Had he or had he not asked what size Foster took in collars? Surely, he could not have done! And yet somehow or other he was sure that the answer had been "eighteen." Disgusting, he had thought it. That anyone could be so fat at any time was unpleasant but at the tail end of a war — and such a war too — it was positively revolting. *I suppose*, he thought, *that he takes half a meal at one restaurant — or what he calls half — and the rest at another — or is he too mean to pay for two?*

Anyhow Foster was eating *pâté maison*. They had brought a great bowl of it and some rolls and they kept on asking you if you had enough when your plate was already full. They always did that, Guy remembered, an amiable trick of the Café Royal's — Oddenino's rather — funny how one could get them muddled up. He made a remark about it to Foster. The heat in this room was very overpowering. Foster seemed rather dim and a long way off. All he said in reply was that the Café Royal and Oddy's were next door to each other and they were both rattling good places anyhow. He would have a little more *pâté maison*, he thought.

"That makes half a pound," Reeves found himself saying out loud. Perhaps it was rather rude, but Foster did not seem to mind it. It was just as Shergold had said, he was so thick-skinned that you could insult him as much as you liked in some ways and yet in others he was as touchy as anything. You never could be quite sure. Reeves took a grip on his thoughts. What was he to talk about? Was he to bring up the troubles of the firm and talk shop at lunch? No. He and Shergold had decided that that was to be done afterwards, when they had got to Foster's flat. Just before…something else was to happen. But there were other things that he, Reeves, wanted to talk to Foster about. A good thing that. Shergold thought he knew everything, but he did not — not this at any rate. It was going to be a surprise to him later — a little later when the centre of the stage was being taken by Reeves, when his first great dramatic moment would be over, and they would come to the second one. Shergold knew about the first, but he did not know about the second and later he would not be in the picture at all. Of course one would keep Cynthia's name out of it. One had to do that. It would be a bit difficult, but somehow it would have to be managed, because there would be a good deal of talk. It could hardly be left out of the newspapers even though newsprint was so short, and even though there was so much other news to put in. Perhaps after all a hint to Shergold would be a good thing. But not a word about the further surprise he had planned. Shergold must know nothing of that. Meanwhile he was failing to look after Foster — not that he needed much attention at the moment beyond the provision of a very small bit of roll upon which to balance a great deal of *pâté maison*.

The scene was getting clearer to Reeves now. Perhaps the effect of the rum had worn off. Or was it something else? It was less like now to what he and Shergold had pictured. He could almost see it now in all the details in which subsequently he was to describe it to two men, one small and dark and one small and fair, who would take a great deal of interest in what he was telling them.

"That claret ought to be here soon," he had begun. "It should go well with the venison."

"Tricky thing to cook, venison," had been Foster's reply. "They do it well here though." His little pig eyes had sunk further into his head at the thought of it. All that pâté had made him red in the face. Perhaps he had eaten too much bread with it. But there would still be room for venison. They gave you very good potatoes with it, he commented, shifting his position slightly on the red plush seat so as to allow more room for his extended stomach.

"Not a pretty picture," Reeves had thought. Later he was to recapture his mood exactly. "But I was not going to let him talk about food all the time. I wanted of course partly to get some information out of him about the Company I manage. Yes, there is another director. Senior to me in theory, but as a matter of fact he is getting rather beyond it. I do all the real work. At least I have since I came back from the war. He was getting it, I found, into rather a muddle, and I was only just beginning to see what was wrong. Oh, nothing serious. Just incompetence. But I can put it right — or could have done." He cleared his throat slightly and seemed to smile at the mistake he had made. The alert intelligent man to whom he was talking had not returned the smile. They seemed to be following closely though. "Or could have done," the dark one echoed. "So you wanted to get some information out of Foster, and you shared a bottle of claret?"

"Yes."

"It was good claret?"

"Oh, not so bad, I think. I hardly seem to remember. I was thinking very hard, you know. Besides, though I wanted Foster to think — and he must have thought, because he was no fool — that I was trying to get him drunk so as to pump him. Of course I had no intention of getting drunk myself and I was sure he had a harder head than mine. Not that I am not pretty capable at that sort of thing myself. Still I saw to it that he had more than his share of the claret. There was no difficulty in that. But perhaps that is the reason why I hardly remember drinking any of it myself."

"I see. You got the information?"

"Not at that time. One would hardly, even with a man like that who knew little of the shades of decent conduct, start by talking shop — and when one was the host too. Besides I wanted to give him a warning, very delicately, about the way he was behaving to a certain lady."

"To…"

"Please understand once and for all that I am not proposing to give you the lady's name. I am telling you everything that it is necessary for you to know, which to my mind is all the more reason why you should confine yourself to the points that I tell you. I have already told you that you are free to take all this down and you have explained my position fully to me."

"Yes, I quite understand. All the same we might not perhaps agree as to what is necessary for us — well, perhaps it is only a formality. But these formalities have to be observed."

"Ridiculous. Once more I repeat that I am telling you everything that you need know. Please confine yourself to what I am telling you. Now, where was I?"

"You were saying that you wished to convey a delicate hint and at the same time you were telling us that you were not going to mention the name of the lady."

"Exactly." A silence fell, and it looked as if Reeves would have to again be prompted. But the alert, dark-haired little man was far too experienced to do that. He knew when to wait and it was not very long before his patience was rewarded.

"Not a nice character — Barry Foster," Reeves went on. "He took — but you must talk to my fellow director about that. He was vindictive. He got a down on my firm, possibly because he never got on with Arthur — Shergold that is. Not perhaps an easy man to get on with, I allow. Too domineering. Quite incapable of appreciating other people's finer points or of realising that other people did work for the company. You see, he had started it and worked it up, I must admit, into quite a flourishing business. When I brought in some extra capital — and some extra brains — he had been making quite a good profit. That was just before the war, only somehow — I never understand these things — those profits never seemed to count when it came to giving us a standard for EPT. Something about the dates, I believe. Do you understand these things?"

A shake of the head had been the only reply. "But you were describing not your fellow director but Foster, and I gathered his behaviour to some lady or other—"

"Was all that it should not be. If there is one thing which I cannot stand it is to see some old man leering at a girl."

"You need not answer me if you would rather not, but I take it you had some particular girl in mind. Wasn't it a young lady to whom you were engaged?"

* * *

UNFORTUNATELY HE WAS NOT. Though it was not for want of trying.

He had decided to allot Easter to the purpose. With the European war ending things were slacker at the factory and the times when you worked right through holidays were over. He could afford to take two or three days. Then spring was early and a walk in the country was exactly what was required. Surely there ought to be some opportunity during it to talk? He suggested it one evening when he and Cynthia were left in the office tidying up a few figures after everyone had gone. "Does a day's walk in the country ever amuse you?" he began.

"Quite a lot," she answered. "Though the very young call it a trifle old-fashioned and murmur things about hags."

"You can confidently exclude yourself from the hag class and risk it. Help you to forget figures and disappointments and people who want to get out costs. Especially the latter."

Cynthia frowned a bit. That was too obvious to be anything but a little tactless. She had no liking for Barry Foster, and she was not going to allow it to be hinted that she had. "I can forget that subject easily," she said. "What day were you thinking of taking a walk? Monday?"

"I thought Sunday. We shall then still have Monday left to get over it."

"Very age conscious, aren't you?"

"Well, perhaps, but as a matter of fact it's I who need the day to recover. Ever since..." he faintly indicated his left hand. For a moment Cynthia looked annoyed and a faint flush appeared on her pretty but rather doll-like face. Both the blush and the pink-and-whiteness of the face were in the habit of annoying her. "As if I were a kid on a magazine cover," she would mutter to herself. But at the moment it was Guy Reeves who was being irritating with his endless playing up of his injury. She looked rather pointedly at his arm and remarked that it would no doubt make him very stiff after a long walk.

The sarcasm was wasted. "Well, one gets no exercise sitting about in this place. Nothing odd about it if we are stiff afterwards and besides one will enjoy doing nothing on Monday after a stroll more than one will doing nothing on Sunday in advance. Can you make it Sunday then?"

"Very well. Trains are poor though. Where had you thought of going?"

For once Guy had had the wit to lay his plans in advance in some detail. He named a train from Waterloo at the reasonable hour of ten-thirty that would take them to Guildford. "And then by Merrow Down to Gomshall and Shere and up through the woods and over to Dorking. There's a train just after half-past five from Dorking North and after that we might have dinner somewhere."

"I see." Cynthia had eyed him a bit narrowly. "Not quite sure about the last part. What about this stiffness?"

"Won't have come on by then."

"And shan't we be in a filthy state?"

"Well, we'll see. Depends how things go."

At that they left it, but Cynthia was rather thoughtful on Saturday evening. On the purely sordid side there was probably money behind Guy Reeves. She did not believe that he had put into the Shergold Engineering Company all of what she gathered had been a fair-sized fortune that he had inherited. A very good thing, she thought, if he had not. It was not a concern she would like to have her all in. Why were the labour costs so high always? There must be something in the continual moans by the Ministry and though Barry Foster was easily satisfied, she was not so sure. Anyhow it was a dreary subject and she would give it no more thought.

For finance was not at all the point. The only thing that mattered was, what did she really think of Guy? In the first place she was sorry for him. He had had to go off to the war leaving behind him a situation that was unsatisfactory in its vagueness. He knew nothing really about Shergold. She always suspected that he had put his money into the business with far too little investigation of his fellow director or of his company. He knew far too little of the engineering side and apparently, he did not propose to learn. It might be all right, but she strongly suspected that it might well lead him into a mess one day. While he had been away there had been nobody really to look after his interests and that she had kept an eye on them had been really her own idea. The very fact that she had carried that out had given her a protective sort of feeling for him. That was the second point.

A very dangerous and false sort of feeling it was, she realised.

For after all, what kind of man was he? He was vain — there was no denying that. He was lazy. That was true too; above all she disliked the way he — to put it crudely — "cashed in" on his injury. She wondered how he came by it. Rather creditably, she gathered from the hints he dropped. But then he would be almost certain to drop exactly that type of hint. She had to admit that to herself, even though the admission made her make a rather wry face. He was good company though, full of infectious gaiety. He would enjoy his walk in Surrey, and he would see to it that she did. If they did have some food together afterwards it would be an entertaining evening and he would not spoil it by petty economies. She sighed as she remembered a rather distressful evening she had once spent with Barry Foster. It was no subject to let her thoughts dwell on, and she dismissed it firmly and settled down to a book before going to bed.

She awoke to find a doubtful morning and she had to take a raincoat with her. It was a bore. It was much nicer to walk without one but at any rate it would serve to put the sandwiches in, which characteristically Guy had arranged she should bring for both of them. It had been rather a business finding anything to make them out of, but with equal characteristic ability she had overcome the difficulties. There was part of her chocolate ration available too and a little plain chocolate would help considerably. She was quite satisfied when she met Guy at the barrier and noted that if he would not take the trouble to do anything about sandwiches, he had at least bought the tickets. "So typical of the helpless male who means well," she said to herself. "Ready to pay but not to take trouble." Out loud she only said, "I wish there was more sun about, but I don't think it will rain. Anyhow not much."

"I shall not allow it to. And if it does, it will only be a shower to freshen one up. I like a bit of air, and anyhow we shall have the wind behind us all day." He had thrown open the window of the carriage as he spoke but the violent protests of an old gentleman at the other end of it forced him to shut it. "He *would*," he whispered to Cynthia, "but you know the rule — 'The stuffy always win'." The whisper was not as inaudible as it should have been.

Cynthia's sympathies were rather with the old gentleman, so she contented herself with a grin. The trivial incident brought Guy closer to her. He would take a bit of handling, she thought. Perhaps too he was not over-considerate.

Merrow Down was soon reached, being nothing like the "hour out from Guildford Town" that Kipling states it to be.

"Nor," said Cynthia, "is the line about 'on Merrow Down the cuckoo's cry, the silence and the sun remain' any more accurate. There is no sign of the sun or the cuckoo. On the other hand silence is not helped by the presence of an Italian prisoner-of-war camp. Don't they look cold?"

"They probably are. Serve them right anyhow. To think that I took those people prisoner in North Africa just so they could spoil the countryside here and eat up all our food."

"Anyhow the blackthorn's out, and there are lots and lots of violets, so let's forget the poor wretches." Cynthia changed the subject. She was glad though when the camp was left behind, and they found themselves on the fringe of a golf course. She would have been walking along happily enough had it not been for her tiresome raincoat. It was too hot going uphill to wear it and if she put it on her arm, it made her arm ache after a while, while if she threw it over her shoulders, it always fell off. Guy's offer to carry it for her would have been more welcome if he had not attached to it various comments and insinuations on the incompetence of women to do things. She stuck to it for herself, being definitely of the opinion that there were some moments when it really was better to cut off your nose to spite your face, and that there were some people who made you do so.

The suspicion of ill-temper on either side hardly lasted a

moment though. If there was a stiff south-west wind, it was anyhow, as Guy had said, behind them and it blew them over downs where the spring was just showing, past copses where the birches were pale green and woods where the chestnut was a brighter green and even the oaks were just beginning to show that curious colour that is almost, but not quite, yellow which young oak leaves seem alone to have. There were cowslips and even in one wood a very early bluebell. There were masses of white anemones being blown about by the wind and if the primroses were unaccountably absent, there was colour in the trees, in the woods, in the hedges and in the grass. *A very suitable setting for the job*, Guy thought. *But I wonder how one sets about proposing to anyone. I suppose one just waits for an opportunity and then gets on with it.* They reached Shere and with hearty appetite ate their sandwiches in a pub. "There is one thing which makes life easier nowadays," Cynthia remarked with her eyes fixed on a tankard, "one is allowed to like beer. No more nonsense about delicate females these days."

"That shrinking modest violet business would not go with a swing now. All the same there must have been a time when women drank beer in old days. After all tea is a comparatively modern idea."

"Oh, brand new — only about a couple of centuries old! Was one completely domesticated all the time in between, do you think?"

"Most of it. I expect there was something to be said for it. Factory work and accounts and all that cannot be very great fun for women, especially if they have a home to look after as well."

"Granted. But what about the women who had neither the one nor the other?"

"I expect they got along somehow." Guy tried to edge the conversation somewhere nearer to the point. They were alone in the saloon bar, and, so far as he could see, the landlord was completely absorbed in the public bar. It was not a very suitable spot perhaps, but possibly not absolutely impossible. "What do you feel, Cynthia, about domestic life? Homes and all that. I mean with the war ending…"

"There may be a chance of some homes being built." Cynthia was determined not to be helpful. What obvious creatures men were! And what a place to choose!

"Yes, quite." Guy felt he was getting on quite well. "People will want to live in them. That sounds a bit fatuous, I know," he went on, catching Cynthia's expression. "But what do you feel about it?"

"About what? Domestic life? Haven't given it a thought!" It was a valiant and discouraging lie.

Guy looked a little depressed. "'I had hoped you had considered…"

"The housing problem in general, you mean? One can hardly help thinking about that. It's being thrust down one's throat every day."

"I didn't mean in general really…"

"Oh, as to myself" (she longed for an interruption. Did no one ever come into this bar?) "I have a perfectly comfortable small flat to live in — and enough to live on."

"But will that last for ever?"

"What — the flat or the income?"

"I really meant the job. Or rather…" he was blundering now, and he knew it, but it was not in his character ever quite to admit it even to himself, "or rather that whole way of living. I mean figures are not everything. One day this whole business of costing may stop."

"That's what Mr Foster—"

"Oh, why drag him in? *Damn* Mr Foster."

"By all means. But he may be right when he says it may stop one day, and after all I was only saying that he agreed with you."

"Do you mean to say that you talked this over with him?"

"No. Not exactly. I have talked over something of the sort with him."

"Really." To her surprise Guy suddenly became taciturn. She had intended to prevent him from getting on too far with any subject that she wished to avoid but apparently, she had done more than that; quite why he seemed to be in such a temper she could not make out, nor was there for the moment any opportunity to find out. Two women, evacuated from London, came in. They were quite unable to talk to any subject but flying bombs. Cynthia and Guy got up and left almost at once.

In the little street of Shere, Guy made one more effort. "Sorry if I jumped down your throat. But I am not really very fond of your talking things like that over with a brute like Barry Foster."

"And why not? He's intelligent — in a way. Especially when it comes to practical facts such as what it costs to live. Besides, is there any reason why I should not talk to him?"

"Oh, none, if you want to! But I should not have thought you would have liked to, that's all."

Cynthia lit a cigarette and hummed to herself:

"'And bears from Shere would come and look For
Taffimai where Shamley stands.'"

It was not a fortunate quotation. "Are you suggesting that I'm a bear?" Guy barked at her.

"I hate being unkind, but really, Guy, why jump down one's throat? Besides I think you are very unfair to Mr Foster. In many ways he is very kind, and I like him quite a lot." Cynthia found herself on the verge of tears, for with her to cry was a regrettable idiosyncrasy which she could never quite master.

After that somehow it was not easy for either of them to get the conversation started again. They began by going up again into the woods, up a steep track and conversation for two people who were neither in quite as good training as they might have been became difficult. Somehow when they got to the top they blundered into a camp. Hidden under the trees along the side of an unexpected road were huts containing detonators and shells and other things unsuitable as an opening to a discussion on married life. Despite the anemones and the spring green there was a weird and uncomfortable atmosphere. It was almost a relief when they blundered into a sentry and were ignominiously turned out. They had to scramble down a steep hill and up another to get on to their road again. Guy felt that he had to mutter some sort of apology for taking her astray, yet he was not best pleased when she forgave him and pointed out that any one of these woods was very like any other. Somehow, she should not, in his opinion, have conveyed the idea that there was anything to forgive or explain away. She should have made it quite clear that there had been no fault on his part at all and that somehow the blame should be attributed to the Army for putting a camp there at all. The clouds darkened and the road down to Dorking seemed longer and longer. Even the belated finding of some primroses did not seem to help matters. Drops of rain began to fall and the exact whereabouts of the station proved elusive. Eventually they reached it. The train was just — but irrevocably — moving out of the station and the rain was just starting in earnest. They could find nowhere to have tea.

In the carriage on the way back, three-quarters of an hour later, Reeves' thoughts were gloomy. Cynthia had already indicated that they would be back too late for any idea of going out anywhere to dinner. She would have to go home and change anyhow. Besides she thought that she had caught a cold.

You would, was Reeves' unspoken comment. *The sort of woman who can discuss the possibility of married life with a man like Foster is just the sort of person who would catch a cold by sitting on a station platform. How on earth the subject was ever raised between them, I simply cannot imagine. Before I go any further, I must find out exactly what has been happening. Unless — unless — this idea that keeps on coming into my head — I wonder where it keeps coming from? But it would make things easier in the end. The ultimate end.*

He set that thought aside and turned back to consider the few remarks that Cynthia had made. There was very little in them. Even he knew in his heart of hearts that he had magnified trivialities. Yet it was odd that she should have tried to evade the subject so carefully when he broached it and yet she had equally clearly "talked it over" with Foster. What right on earth had she to compare Foster's opinion with his? As if Foster knew anything about it or as if he had an opinion worth considering at all! And then there was that "I like him quite a lot." That would never do! He must talk it over with Shergold, at least not exactly that, but he would find out whether Shergold had noticed anything between Cynthia and Barry Foster. A good fellow, Shergold, in some ways, if not in others. At any rate he had a very shrewd idea of Foster's character.

* * *

"An unpleasant character," was Shergold's invariable comment. As he and Reeves sat in their office on that hot Wednesday of April 18th, he had no doubt about it and he clearly did not intend to let Reeves have any either. "It was exactly like him to eat all that lunch. Infernally expensive too. He was probably actually pleased at that."

"That's because you are mean, and he knew it," Reeves grunted. "Anyhow one had to do him properly first. Besides I keep on telling you that all I remember is the second rum cocktail."

"So you said before. Do get on with it. It's not the kind of subject that improves by beating about the bush."

"Isn't that a mixed metaphor?"

"Never mind if it is. Did he go back to his flat quietly?"

"Of course he did. I didn't get him drunk so that he was dancing and singing. He just went back by bus."

"A number sixty bus."

"I suppose so. I believe he paid for the tickets. So I suppose I must have got him a bit drunk. Or did I get a bit drunk myself because, for the life of me, I cannot remember? Nor am I really sure what the flat looked like."

"Pull yourself together — and please remember that you have got to know. If you start contradicting yourself, there is no knowing where you will get to."

"I have a pretty good idea where you think I shall get to anyhow." For some reason best known to himself a grin spread over Reeves' good-looking face.

"Perhaps; but if you get it wrong, you will not do yourself justice. It is essential — it is only fair to yourself that you should make the right effect."

The grin came off abruptly. "And I'm going to. Make no mistake like that. I shall be an absolute marvel to everyone."

"I know. Everyone will admire you. They will have to recognise your calmness — your courage."

"Everyone. I wish I could have my old colonel here! He wants a lesson teaching to him." For once he flushed, and not with pride, as he looked at his left hand. The remarks of his commanding officer, he had heard afterwards, had altogether lacked the appreciation that was his due. The man had even started to suggest that it was an unusual and all too convenient wound. "It was a damnable lie," he muttered practically inaudibly. He let his thoughts run on. No one had ever understood him. No one.

Shergold seemed to divine what was in his mind. "But now they are going to appreciate what you have done. If you get it right, that is. I think I can see the scene. Let me run over it with you." As Reeves made no answer, the older man sat down opposite to him and began to talk slowly in rather a monotonous voice, as if he was anxious to be certain that Reeves fully took in every point. "Foster was rather cross at paying for the tickets and when you came to get off the bus, he made some little play with putting them ostentatiously into the box, by way of reminding you that you had so far forgotten yourself as to let him pay. Then you crossed the road. The entrance to his block of flats was only a few yards off Maida Vale. They are not a very modern block of flats — outside they are rather ugly red brick."

"Damnably ugly," Reeves echoed. "But comfortable inside."

"Yes, quite comfortable inside."

"Trust Foster for that."

"There is a lift opposite to you as you go in. Perhaps a porter in peace time but as it is automatic it does not really matter. You are not quite sure of which floor his flat is on, but you think it is on the third floor."

"Why shouldn't I be sure? I've been there, haven't I?"

"You have been there. The flat is on the third floor. You went up to it in a lift. He opened the door with a latch-key."

"How the hell do you know?"

"He would do so naturally. As for the rest, it is all in the post office telephone directory. Besides I had a look at it once."

"Very well then." Despite his closed eyes, Reeves seemed to be listening intently.

"He showed you into a little hall from which two doors led, one a bit to the left you thought was his bedroom. There was a bathroom at the end of the passage on your left. The other door was on your right and you went through that into his sitting room. Now get the sitting room right."

The tale was taken up by Reeves. "An ordinary sized and shaped room, the proportions like a piece of notepaper with the door at the bottom left corner, a gas fire in the wall on your left — thank heavens he did not insist on lighting it — an easy chair in front of it on the other side of the fireplace, a window on the wall opposite, a bookcase at the far end on your left." He stopped and seemed to find difficulty in going on.

"There was one other chair in the room — a writing chair by the table underneath the window. You took the easy chair."

"How the hell do you know that?"

"You would — I mean," Shergold corrected himself quickly, "he would naturally give it to a guest."

"That's all you know about Barry Foster, or me either for that matter. I took the chair at the writing table. I could talk to him better that way."

"And you talked very freely — and at some considerable length?"

"I did. First of all I dealt with a private affair of my own. There's no need to look at me like that. I suppose I could if I wanted to, couldn't I? And anyhow what the dickens has it got to do with you? Nothing at all. I am not going to talk about it to you or to anyone else either now or later." His attention seemed to wander and instead of Barry Foster's flat he saw in his mind's eye the saloon bar at Shere.

"Just as you like." Shergold had a fairly good idea of the situation and apparently, he was quite content to leave it at that. "You talked about the firm."

"I did." The remark brought Reeves back from his reverie. "I told him all the things that we had talked over a great many times and accused him roundly of having milked the business till it would stand no more. I know very little about accounts, old man, but it is pretty clear even to an amateur like myself that something is wrong. Everyone says the same thing, even Cynthia Trent started hinting at it."

"Oh! Miss Trent did, did she?"

"Well, not so definitely as that. She just said that labour costs seemed to her a bit high, but of course I never let her talk about it for long. Not good for little girls like her to interfere with grown-up affairs."

There was no doubt that Shergold agreed with him as to that, but once more he brought Reeves' attention back to the point with a question as to Foster. Reeves' reply was quick: "Oh! Yes, of course I put it to him perfectly clearly. If there was anything wrong, it was his business to know that it was wrong. If there was nothing wrong, why did everybody—"

"Everybody?"

"Well, the Ministry — say that there was something wrong? 'Those chaps,' I said, 'know a thing or two. It is fashionable, I know, to say that all civil servants are dead from the waist up, but they are not — I'll say they are not. And when they start raising the kind of enquiries that it seems they have been raising, you can be pretty sure that there is something wrong. They may go to sleep for months on end but when they wake up it is to some purpose.' On that he referred me to you, a dirty way of dodging his own dirty work to my mind. He said that you kept the wages book and that you knew everything that was paid out and that if I wanted to know anything about that side of the business, I had better ask you. Do you know that he even insinuated that if there was anything wrong, I had better see what you had been doing?"

"I suppose he had to put you off somehow or start some red herring or other."

"Quite, and if I had not talked this over with you beforehand, he might have succeeded, but as it was, I was not going to be led astray that way. 'If there was anything,' I went on, 'it would be you, not Shergold, who ought to know about it. So far as I understand the matter it is exactly what the Ministry pay you to know about.' 'Well, hardly — or at any rate not only,' he said, and do you know he began to talk about all sorts of other things that he says he has to do. Mere accountancy nonsense, leading to no good as usual. In fact he said exactly all the things you said that he would. So I went back to the point again. You kept the wages books I knew, but he did what the Ministry told him, saw the

Insurance Cards and that the total of the book went into our accounts books. If he had done that there would be nothing that you could have done wrong. I have a sort of idea that I had him there because I fancy that I detected a blush. I wonder if he did all that he ought to do?"

"He did. Be quite sure about that. There is no need to go into all that again — for anyone. Don't let your imagination run away with you."

The slight implied criticism and instantly had Reeves up in arms. "I have a very vivid imagination — very vivid indeed, but I never let it run away with me. Never."

"Quite." Shergold commented drily.

"Well, let that be understood then. Where was I?" He idly, and without apparent comprehension, examined the component part that the Shergold Engineering Company had hoped to machine in quantity.

Shergold took up the tale. "He had assured you that he knew perfectly well that our books and accounts were perfectly in order and that he had made carefully all proper checks and satisfied himself fully."

Reeves hesitated. "I suppose he did say all that."

"He must have done. He had done so; you know. Besides that is in effect what you told me."

"Well, if you say so. Of course I was not in a position to argue with him then any more than I am with you, so I turned the point on him very cleverly — just as we had agreed that I would — 'very well,' I said, 'if you are so sure that everything is right, when in fact' (and I was very emphatic about it), 'when in fact there is obviously something wrong, there can be only one excuse. You must be in the wrong yourself. Now, my fellow director' (you, you know) 'hardly seems to understand the point. He is very stupid of course.' (I had to say that, because I did not want him to know that you had told me about the way he was blackmailing you into paying him large sums out of the business.) Besides it's true — you are pretty stupid." Reeves seemed to be unaware that he was not being absolutely polite and went on blandly, "so I laughed it off with a joke about everyone who always sat in a frightful atmosphere without a breath of air being bound to be a bit wooden-headed and went back to the point. Finally I charged him fairly and squarely with what we know he has done and explained to him how he did it. That seemed to surprise him a bit. Finally I told him that I knew exactly the sum that had been taken from the firm and I told him that we expected him to pay it back."

Shergold laughed. "What a hope! It was exactly his weak point. Besides I am perfectly sure that he had spent it all long ago. But of course he did not show any signs of falling in with that idea."

"None whatever. We never thought he would. In fact he made a perfectly revolting suggestion."

"Which was?"

"Oh, never mind."

"But I do mind." Shergold got up and leant over the table so that his face was quite close to Reeves. "I think it would be wiser if you told me, even though I shall know nothing of it later and even though you will remember that I never knew anything of it."

"Oh very well. All the same though, I had made up my mind that I would not talk about it. It concerned — it concerned someone else."

"I think I understand." Shergold sat down again but his gaze never left Reeves' face. "Though how you are going to explain that away, shall we say, later, I hardly know. Still it is entirely your affair. I shall not be concerned at all."

"You leave that to me. And as for mentioning that *you* had any knowledge of my intentions, set your mind at rest. This is a matter in which I take all the credit. So far you have left everything to me, you who let it all happen, let the mess occur, you expect me to put it all right. But that's the way things always happen. I have to do all the work and then people make," he stretched out his left hand and looked at it pointedly, "insinuations."

"More than insinuations this time, I fancy," Shergold said quietly, "but go on." Never having met Reeves' former commanding officer he had no idea of what the insinuations were to which reference was being made.

But Reeves was up again in the air, "Insinuations will *not* be made. I shall be doing the talking myself, and for once people will understand — fully."

"Without explaining this last point? Will they think that there was enough, shall we say, reason?"

"That will be my affair. I do not imagine that I shall have any difficulty in convincing them and besides I believe they do not concern themselves primarily with what you call 'reasons.'"

"Go on." Shergold was tense now and he appeared to be in a hurry. He looked at his watch.

"I was not going to stand for Foster's filthy suggestions. I had always wondered beforehand when I thought it over whether, when it came to the point, I should have the courage. I ought never to have doubted. Of course I should always have had the courage. I always have it when it is necessary. But that final remark stirred me on. I jumped up from the chair of the writing table where I had been sitting and I went behind that fat, loathsome, insinuating toad and with the thumb and the first finger of my left hand—"

Shergold's surprise was such that he jumped up, "With your *left* hand. I had always thought — I mean I know how wonderful you are with your left hand, marvellous, but surely it would not be the natural thing — surely you mean your right hand?"

Very languorously Reeves stretched out his left hand. "No, I was always very left-handed and though I hold that any good man should be a bit ambidextrous, still I prefer using my left hand — it gives me a feeling of satisfaction. People think that it is an infirmity to have lost three fingers, but I like to demonstrate to them that it is an advantage."

"I know you could do almost anything with your left hand, but surely you would not have liked to have risked it in this case?"

"I took no risk. I came up from behind him and I seized his windpipe with my thumb and first finger held up vertically and then to make sure — doubly sure — I brought my right hand into play too and I used it just to apply, shall we say, a little gentle pressure to my left hand. He did not struggle — much. In fact I think he was rather surprised."

Shergold gave a slight shudder. "He had some right to be sur—"

"Don't you believe me," Reeves suddenly shot at him.

"Of course I do. I know how carefully you thought it out and how reliable your accuracy is. But I always imagined you going for him with the right hand, openly, from in front."

"Are you suggesting that it was cowardly to come from behind?"

"Not a bit." Shergold was nervously placatory. "Anyone else would, but you — you are such an exception to the general rule. An ordinary person might not have had the strength in his left hand." He looked down at his own and nervously clenched and unclenched his fingers. "It makes it all so, how shall I put it? So personal to you — now with the right hand—"

"That is my affair. I wanted it to be personal to me." Shergold still looked down at his hand. "Your finger and thumb placed vertically? Then the rest of your hand would not come into play at all?"

"I thought that you were aware that I had no other fingers to my hand."

"That is not what I mean. I only mean that I should have thought that if you held your hand so to speak horizontally, you would be able to use all the bit in between your thumb and the first finger — all the lower joints of them and so would get greater pressure more easily."

"That just shows how little you know about it. I do things my own way and as I have already said I wanted the whole thing to be personal to me — to be quite incapable of being imitated. And so please leave me to carry out my own affairs my own way for the next act is about to begin." He rose to his feet dramatically as if he were facing an imaginary audience. "I am now going to write to Scotland Yard and give them a very interesting thrill. At first it will seem very ordinary to them. It is only as it unfolds that they will realise that there is something unusual, something so remarkable that they have never heard of anything of the sort before, that they are dealing with an exceptional person of real intelligence and courage. I think it will interest even them." He sat down suddenly and seized a piece of paper. "I shall write to them."

"I should have thought it would be more interesting to go round and watch their faces."

"No. I shall write I tell you." His pen started to move over the paper. Then he stopped suddenly and seemed to hesitate. "I feel infernally sleepy," he said unexpectedly.

"The natural reaction after all you have been through. I should advise you to wait a bit. Even — though it seems an extraordinary suggestion — to lie down for a while before you write to them — or go round to them."

"I shall write," Reeves' voice was dreamy. "This afternoon at — when the devil was the time? I'm all in a muddle about the time. Anyhow this afternoon," his pen scratched the paper slowly, "I murd — I say, how do you spell 'murdered'?"

"You see," said Shergold. "You are not at your absolute best. And you need to be — even *you* need to be, your very absolute best. Just rest in the room next door. A few minutes will make all the difference. Most natural thing in the world to do.

Anybody else would have collapsed long ago instead of coming back to the office and telling me all about it."

Reeves yawned again. "I wanted to be...sure I had it right. I can remember nothing about the journey back though."

"Of course not. There's a bed still next door. Foster can keep for a while." Rather slowly he helped Reeves out of the chair. "By the way," he said, almost casually, "I suppose you are quite certain that he is dead?"

"Oh, perfectly! What do you take me for? I pressed and pressed and..." He was almost asleep as he reached the bed.

PART II

"And when the barbarians saw the *venomous* beast hang on his hand, they said among themselves: No doubt this man is a murderer."

— ACTS OF THE APOSTLES 28.4.

To anyone who has not accustomed himself fully to the habit of confessing to the crime of murder, Scotland Yard seems a formidable place. You could not — at any rate on occasion in war time — walk in from the Embankment with the cheerful bustle of trams and the river to help you. You had to come in from the Whitehall side down a roadway that was not designed to enhance the drama, if it were drama that your action sought.

Moreover there was a large and elderly uniformed constable on the day in question at the actual entrance to the yard, hovering about, present and yet not obtrusively present. It was doubtful if you had to ask leave to go in from him or not. Reeves went up to him, hesitated, and turned away as if after all he was really wanting to see what time it was according to Big Ben. It was about ten minutes to five he noticed. The street was full of men in khaki, mostly Canadians and Americans, mentally recording the fact that they had seen the Houses of Parliament. Good news had sold the evening papers out. The European war — and with a shock he realised that he had forgotten its existence — was rapidly reaching its end.

For a moment he wavered. Why should he not have peace too? Then he remembered that the matter was done and that, though he was not going to mention the fact, he had told Shergold all about it. There was nothing for it but to play the role he had allotted to himself and play it well! He went back to where the policeman loitered by the gate. Whether access was going to be denied to him or not, he was not sure, but he was not going to chance it. It would be a poor start to be stopped on the way in and so he began the conversation himself. "I want," he said, "to see — well, I suppose it would be the detective inspector on duty." He cursed himself mentally for having overlooked the point of who it was that he required.

The constable looked a little doubtful. "The detective inspector—? With what object, sir?"

"I want..." Reeves had drawn himself up to his full height now. It was regrettable that there was practically no audience at all. Then he paused in the vain hope of increasing the effect. The whole thing was being an anti-climax so far. What a mistake he had made in accepting Shergold's suggestion that he should go round himself! He ought to have followed his own first idea and written, so that the setting would be fixed, and the action carried out by the police. But then there was that difficulty in orthography. To confess to a crime and spell it wrong! No. He was right to have come. He was sure that he was right.

"You wanted?" Constable Yarrow prompted solidly.

"I wanted..." But no, the constable was not of sufficient importance to receive the information that he wished to give. "I want to talk to someone in authority."

"If you would let me know the nature of the matter?"

Reeves was furious. Why should this elderly and blundering subordinate ruin the situation? What business was it of his? But there it was. There was apparently no way of getting round Constable Yarrow's stolidity. There was nothing for it but to make the best of the situation, such as it was. He had been a fool, perhaps, to ask for somebody of whose existence he did not know. Moreover he should not have gone for such small game. He should have gone to the top from the start. Too late, as he felt it to be, he tried to remedy the error. Once more he drew himself up to his full height (but as the constable was if anything a quarter of an inch taller this was not so effective as it might have been) and he struck an attitude almost physically. "I wish to inform the Chief Commissioner for Police that this afternoon at about three o'clock, anyhow between two-thirty and three-thirty, I murdered Mr Barry Foster of 32 Maida Vale Mansions."

Constable Yarrow was apparently used to such openings. "Really, sir? I doubt as how the Chief Commissioner is in this very moment." He appeared to be wondering whether he should suggest to Guy that he took a little walk and thought it over. But if he had any real idea of making such a suggestion he was overwhelmed by Reeves. "Is that all you can say about it? You appear, Constable, to treat the matter with a levity which I can assure you will do you little good with your superiors." He began to warm to the work in hand. This was wholly better, even if it was not exactly as he had imagined it to be. There was opposition to be overcome and with the presence of opposition his spirits rose. Gone wholly was the wish that he had written to Scotland Yard, gone too was any hesitation. He would go through with it now, however difficult it might be to get the idea into the heads of any mere constable, however long the delays and however vexatious the obstructions were.

"Levity, sir? Not at all, sir." Constable Yarrow believed in perfect courtesy always. It had not, it was true, got him very far, but, on the whole, it had made life more comfortable. "If you would step this way, sir, we will soon get your little business fixed up. At least," he corrected himself hurriedly as Reeves apparently did not like the word "little," "we can get the matter settled." The alteration seemed to be hardly an improvement and he took refuge in silence.

Silence too was shortly to be Reeves' fate. A few questions from a man in plain clothes covering only the most elementary points were all that was at first vouchsafed to him. Then he was left alone in a small room, a waiting room, he imagined, for what at first seemed to him to be an unconscionably long time. Once more he ran over in his mind the story that he was to tell. It was a good and convincing story, he thought, and there was yet an opportunity to retrieve the present situation of partial bathos. In fact now he came to think of it, he had always expected some such period of bathos. His moment was to come. Perhaps too, even now, he was the subject of more observation than he realised.

The idea that perhaps unseen eyes were watching him through unexpected chinks in walls or doors was a fascinating one to him. He braced himself up and sat in an attitude that he considered to be worthy of himself. He found himself smiling and carefully removed the traces of so doing. The very slightest trace of an appearance of satisfied pleasure would be one that he would be glad to give but only the very slightest. He feared that someone might describe it as "a grin" or "a leer" and neither of those descriptions could he stand, especially the former. He was not a vapouring attitudinising idiot. He was primarily the apparent instrument of justice, though before they had finished, they would find that he was in fact something more than that. Moreover he was a very unusual man and he was going to carry the situation through with unerring dignity. It was only worth doing if he could achieve that. The conception helped him to sit on a rather hard wooden bench with more tranquillity and patience than he would otherwise have achieved. Moreover, rather belatedly, he noticed a glass partition in one part of the room. He was right then. He could if necessary be observed and he rather thought that he was.

It is at least doubtful if he would have been able to preserve his equanimity had he been able to hear the preliminary conversation going on elsewhere in the same building between Detective Inspector Hardwick and Detective Sergeant Matthews. It had been begun, as so many conversations between the two of them had been begun, by Matthews putting his head just inside the door of Hardwick's room. It was a habit that particularly annoyed Hardwick as indeed did many other things done by Matthews, a capable man with brains and ability but so modest and superficially, at least, distrustful of himself and frightened of giving offence that he had got into the habit of behaving in a cringing way that Hardwick could not stand. He liked his subordinates to be confident without being over-confident, to defer to him without kowtowing and he did not like them to behave like worms, and there were moments when no one could deny that Matthews did behave, at any rate, like a worm. In consequence Hardwick was apt to be sharp with him with the inevitable and unwanted result that Matthews only cringed the more. This trick of putting only his head into a room was an old one and had, Hardwick thought, been stopped. "Do come right in, Matthews, I have asked you before not to poke your head in only."

"Sorry, sir. But there is no need to worry you for more than a few minutes." Matthews came right in and apologetically tugged his tie. It was beginning to fray and the dark blue suit that he wore was very definitely shiny, but there it was. His wife needed all his coupons for the youngster and anyhow this blue suit had been a good one. It suited his fair hair, carefully brushed back, his rosy face and his blue grey eyes. If he got a new one it might not suit so well, and it would certainly be of inferior material and vastly greater price.

But his mind was brought back from the subject of clothes' rationing by Hardwick's brusque enquiry. "What is it then? I am pretty busy."

"I just wanted to tell you that another of the people who insist on confessing to a murder has just come in."

"As mad as most, I suppose. Why worry me with this?"

"Because I am not sure he is so mad. He looks a bit certain of himself without overdoing it either, so it may not be wholly imaginary. Moreover it is not a murder that we have reported. Confessions generally come from people reading the papers."

"I know. You have sent someone to look into it?"

"Detective Constable Troughton and another man are on their way now. If there is anything in it shall I come back and report further to you, sir?"

"Oh very well, but really, Matthews, make up your mind a bit about it first, will you?"

"Certainly, sir." Matthews looked a little pained.

"And start the usual preliminary enquiries."

"Naturally, sir. But I was wondering — supposing there is something in it — will you hear what the man wants to say with me, sir. It's getting a bit late and I thought you might…" He trailed off leaving the impression that the obvious conclusion of the sentence implied that Hardwick's departure for the day ought to be later than it would be — a proposition that was wholly inaccurate.

"He wants to make a statement, does he?"

"He is simply bursting to make a statement. In fact I rather gather that he would prefer to make a broadcast. He would have to hurry a bit to be in time for the six o'clock news though. Besides with all this war news…"

"It sounds as if he were a very ordinary type!" A joke from Matthews was rare and Hardwick was sorry to find that he had rather snubbed him.

"Oh quite ordinary, if it is wholly untrue. We have plenty of those who imagine things, but when they have actually done things, they are seldom so pleased about it. It takes an unusual man to be pleased with confessing to a murder that he has in fact done."

"You think that in reality he has?"

"Might have."

"Very well then. When Troughton lets you know anything and if there does seem to be something into which to enquire, I shall be here." Hardwick suppressed the giving of thanks whose receipt he cordially disliked and turned back to the reading of some other papers. His leg swung to and fro, to and fro, a trick in which he always indulged to assist concentration. It was one which Matthews hated. He could never take his eyes off the swinging leg and it always put him out of his stride. Yet he could not but admire Hardwick. For one thing he had a memory that was absolutely infallible, a very considerable professional advantage. For another, while he was keen and penetrating, he was also absolutely just, and if, for a moment or so, he could be sharp with subordinates, he would always be fair in the end. If there was any credit going, it would come to the man who deserved it whether the man was Inspector Hardwick or not.

It was not long before Troughton was reporting on the telephone. He had effected an entrance into 32 Maida Vale Mansions. In it he had found the body of a man. He had not of course touched the body but at a guess he would say that strangling was quite likely to be the cause of death. He could see no other cause. From the evidence of papers lying visible on the table, the man's name was Foster, and he was clearly employed by one of the Government departments. There were figures on the table dealing with a company called the Shergold Engineering Company Ltd. Possibly the deceased had been writing a report on them to the Ministry. Yes. They would wait where they were until Sergeant Matthews arrived himself or gave him further orders. Would the police surgeon be round soon? Detective Constable Troughton had sighed when he was told that owing to war-time exigencies there was difficulty about getting hold of a doctor and that Sergeant Matthews had first of all to take a statement. It was after half-past five and he had hoped to get back to his tea soon after half-past six. He did not however sigh very deeply. Those in his profession, even in war time, had to take their meals when they could. But it was infernally hot, and he wished that he could disturb the room to the extent of opening a window. At the last moment Sergeant Matthews relieved at least his boredom by telling him to get on to the Ministry and give them the information of the death of their employee.

It was not, however, a remarkably interesting conversation for if Troughton was not so interested in Foster as he might have been — and somehow, he had not taken a liking to the face of the man who was slumped in the chair by the fireplace. Perhaps he had not made enough allowance for the fact that the man was not looking his best — the official at the Ministry with whom at last he made contact seemed even more bored.

"Establishments Branch speaking." The voice had sounded quite live at first.

"Scotland Yard here." (Well, if the Ministry liked to talk that way, he could do it too.)

"Oh, yes?" There was a gentle implication that the Ministry had heard of the Yard.

"You employ a Mr Foster — a Mr Barry Foster."

"Very possibly. We employ quite a lot of people, you know."

"We have reason to think — but I am instructed to ask you to keep this matter to yourself if you would be so good — that he was murdered this afternoon. At any rate he is dead."

"Really?" Establishments Branch was quite unruffled. Apparently, members of the staff of the Ministry were murdered frequently, especially in the afternoon. "Foster, did you say? I must put his name in the appointments list."

"Appointments?" It did not seem to Troughton that many more appointments were likely to go the way of Barry Foster.

"Yes. But with a note 'deceased' beside his name. We usually abbreviate it. That is so that the vacancy can be filled if necessary. They may decide not to, of course, as it is so late in the war — the European war, I should say." He corrected himself with meticulous accuracy and went on to point out that they had many Fosters. In what branch was this particular Foster?

That was a question which Troughton could not answer. He had understood however that the man was an accountant, employed in investigating the charges made by firms for the work they did. "I may be wrong, sir," he went on, "but that is the idea. I have got from his papers."

"An accountant? Oh yes. I thank you very much. That will help me to find out who he is. I expect the Director of Contracts may be interested. Would you like me to tell him?"

"I expect that would be right, sir. If you would just pass it on confidential like. Possibly too, sir, we may want to know something of what work he was actually engaged on at the time. In that case, sir, whom should I talk to?"

"Let me think. Possibly — no, I think it would be best if you would talk to me in the first instance. In case there is some confusion as to his identity and where he was employed in the Ministry. I will find out about him and be able to give you the telephone number and name of the man to whom you should talk. There is just one thing though, I have accepted your statement on the phone without confirmation, we should require rather more proof of who you are. I am sure you can understand that."

"Quite, sir. That would be supplied." As Troughton received the Ministry's thanks and put the telephone down it dawned on him that he had derived no information from the Ministry whatever. He rather took off his hat to them. "But they do seem to take that chap's death blasted calmly," he said to his colleague.

* * *

LATER ON, when Foster's death was fully established, the Ministry were not to take his death so calmly. Or at any rate Mr Pennington was not to do so. But then Mr Pennington had had the misfortune to have Barry Foster working under him for some years. Privately he had nicknamed him 'V1' from his habit of announcing his arrival from some way off with fussy self-importance and of detonating violently in the office if anyone was so rash as to suggest for a moment that anything that he had done was not perfect.

And now apparently the fellow had got himself killed at a particularly awkward time. It would be a nuisance to take on anyone else so late in the war to take over his work and yet there was still just as much work to do as ever. Moreover he had got killed in a particularly public way and no Ministry courts the publicity which may well arise from one of its staff getting himself murdered. "Fortunate thing it is not a woman though, who has been liquidated," thought Pennington. "They talk about them even more. Finally Foster must needs go and get bumped off apparently in some way connected with Shergold Engineering; at any rate with papers about that beastly company all over his desk. If there is going to be any trouble about that outfit, I think that I had better know absolutely all about it."

Fortunately for himself, he was already pretty fairly well up in the history of the company, so far as it affected the Ministry. He had had to look into the reports on them only recently in response to a suggestion from above that the company's prices were too high, and he was only too well aware of the violent reaction to defend them which had been Foster's almost automatic response. Criticism of them he had regarded, as he always did with any company whose accounts he had investigated, as a definite and personal insult. As for criticising his reports, Foster practically always got into a state of nervous fury if anyone even read them. He had recently developed a technique for saying, "No doubt they are all wrong. I never pretended to be a good accountant. I hope I am a little bit above *that*. But at any rate they embody a good settlement and if you go back to the company and raise these points, even though you may be right, you will only get a worse settlement. So make up your mind to that and for heaven's sake leave the thing alone. After all it is not as if we are not months behindhand with our work." Moreover Pennington had found that if he had insisted, the various companies had in fact raised unexpected and rather novel points. He was very strongly of the opinion that the ingenuity had occasionally been Foster's and not the companies.

Still there it was. Foster was dead and apparently was going to be almost as much of a nuisance dead as he had been living and it was very necessary to read once more through all the reports on the Shergold Engineering Company that Foster had sent in. Pennington sighed. He had so nearly transferred the work to someone else on several occasions and how he wished he had. An examination by a second person would have been so very helpful. It would at the least have sounded so much better.

There was one thing about them though. The reports were in order. As he read one after the other, Pennington began to be encouraged. They were quite presentable, apart from the handwriting which was revoltingly careless. Also, and equally careless, there was an odd mistake here and there, but it was always in something that did not matter — a typical Foster performance which he remembered thinking at the time had not been worth querying. Now that it was necessary the adjustments were easy to make. On the whole they were a steady and useful set of reports. It might be a good thing to type them perhaps, in case they were ever asked for. Typists were scarce, but still perhaps it would be as well to do it. They would look so much better. With those to support him he could face any enquiry. There was nothing wrong that he could see, except that there was just this point that the labour costs were so often said to be high. He made a note of what they had been, and he started looking in the files as to other companies with the object of making a comparison.

But comparisons were not so easy to make as might be thought. In placing their contracts the Ministry had found that they had to use many companies — in fact dispersion had been a necessary precaution owing to air bombardment. Consequently one company would very seldom make some store throughout. They would sub-contract a part here and a part there and the parts that they would sub-contract would not always be the same one. Some too would be given the partially constructed item as a free issue. Others would buy it. The differences were innumerable, the similarities few and even when they did exist there were further difficulties in that the complaint of extravagance was in connection with the labour charged direct to the job and that never meant the same as between any two companies. One for instance would put their foreman direct, and another would put them into overheads. There were similar discrepancies of method as to overtime and so on and so forth.

"The plain fact of it is," eventually said Pennington to himself, "that a technical man who knew these jobs from an engineering point of view would say he could tell if the amount charged was too high or not, but I very much doubt whether he would stand up to cross-examination and I certainly do not think that he could prove it, though if I ask them now they will all say that they can. From an accountancy point of view I can prove nothing. All the same I think that I had better go and see this firm myself and go into the question of their method of charging things. These reports of Foster's look all right but I have an uneasy suspicion that he might have scamped his job somewhere and a still more uneasy feeling that he might have been bluffed. Meanwhile I think that a look at the Somerset House files to see what the past history of the company is might be useful. I wonder who is free to go and do that now? Or will I go and do it myself? On the whole I think that I'll do it myself. So here goes."

His journey to Bush House however was not very fruitful. He found the Shergold Engineering Company to be a private limited company with two directors. All this was exactly as in Foster's report. As to shareholding, Shergold had had more shares than Reeves but there were two other shareholders whose holdings were small but who could, if they both united with Reeves, outvote Shergold. It was necessary though that both should be in agreement with Reeves. It seemed to Pennington to be an interesting way of preserving the rights of Reeves as a minority shareholder, if that were the idea. Yet, except in an extreme case, it really left Shergold in virtual control, provided he had the ability. From what Foster had told him, Pennington believed that the ability was most certainly there. For the rest, Shergold had started the company as was obvious from its name. He had converted the business that he had into a company about a year before the war started and he had obtained his shares by putting in the assets of his previous firm. The new capital for the company had come from Reeves and if Pennington read a complicated agreement correctly, Reeves had paid Shergold a cash consideration as well. It looked just possible that the bargain had not been a disadvantageous one for Shergold, that he had got out most, or all of the money that he had put in originally to the firm and still retained practically a majority shareholding in the company. Beyond that there did not seem to be any objection that could be raised.

* * *

EARLIER ON THAT hot Wednesday afternoon, Detective Sergeant Matthews too had been getting over his objections. He was even beginning to overcome those of Inspector Hardwick. "At any rate, sir, I think we must hold him."

"Because?"

"Because he is the first person to tell us of Foster's murder. Troughton says that there was no sign of the door of Foster's flat having been forced and if Reeves was not the last person there, who was? Moreover the very short account that he has given us so far has not been proved to be inaccurate as yet. Of course we are only just beginning to check up on it."

"Naturally." Hardwick almost snubbed Matthews with the incisiveness of the word. Of course they were only just beginning to check up! But why say so to Hardwick of all people?" I suppose that what you want to recommend is that we jointly take a full statement from Reeves now?"

"Please. Do you think that we had better caution him first?"

"In view of your remark that you think we ought to hold him, I imagine that you recommend that?"

"Please."

"I suppose that means 'yes'." Hardwick sat in his favourite attitude, slightly askew to his table. One leg was crossed over the other and was swinging gaily to and fro. He was inclined not to trust Matthews' judgment, on this occasion, but that was only because he did not believe in people who gave themselves up. A silly thing to do, it seemed to him. In his experience murderers were many kinds of things that they ought not to be, but they were not fools. "We shall have to check up what he says very carefully."

"Fifty-eight, fifty-nine — I beg your pardon." Matthews blushed violently and took his gaze off the swinging leg whose swinging's back to forward he had been counting. They had very nearly hypnotised him.

"What *are* you talking about?"

"I was thinking…thinking that we should have to account for every second of Reeves' time." It was all that he could think of to account for the numbers and, thin though it sounded to him, it was apparently accepted for Hardwick answered without further comment, "If he gives a detailed and accurate account of his movements, we shall. From the little we know of him, I rather think that the discrepancies will be more noticeable than the accuracy. But we must of course carry out the usual routine, namely, to look into Foster's movements and find out who had the opportunity to kill him."

"Quite, sir. And you will caution this man Reeves?"

"I think so. It sounds as if he were the type of man who will insist on talking anyhow, so it is not likely to do us any harm and it may make things easier afterwards." Matthews tactlessly looked a little shocked. It was not exactly what he would have admitted to be the object of caution. Perhaps Hardwick too was aware of the point for he went on, "Besides it's only fair. If he *will* talk, he must take the consequences, but at least he ought to be warned. I confess to you that in my heart of hearts I shall not believe a single word he says…"

"Apparently he is anxious to be overwhelmingly convincing."

"Well, all the more reason for warning him. But he will have to prove it. Bring him in."

The summons was nectar to Reeves. In the waiting room he had begun to wilt, but now at last he was to be taken seriously. He walked into Hardwick's room with an air and calmly looked round. It was much as he expected; a very plain and unornamented office, the furniture utilitarian, the walls distempered. Detective Inspector Hardwick too was more or less what he had pictured, except that he was disappointingly small — small men, in Reeves' opinion had an unfair advantage. One could not bully them.

For a moment he had continued to look round the room calmly. He was glad to see that there was a certain amount of window open. The waiting room had been airless and had reminded him of Shergold's ceaseless insistence on having every window shut always. His mind began to wander and to bring before him the looks and even the tones of voice of his fellow director; the very phrases that Shergold used were running in his brain. It was all exactly as Reeves had expected it to be, except for an inexplicable feeling of hunger. He was called to his senses by Hardwick's quiet voice suggesting that he should sit down. He was not surprised to find that he was facing the light, nor that the chair was hard.

"I am Detective Inspector Hardwick," the man on the other side of the table began. "This is Detective Sergeant Matthews." He pointed to the fair-haired man now sitting at a table before the wall with a pencil in his hand and a note book in front of him. "I understand that you wish to make a statement as to the death of a Mr Barry Foster of 32 Maida Vale Mansions. It is my duty to inform you that you are entitled to have any legal assistance that you may require and that you are under no obligation to make a statement on the subject, but that if you do so such statement will be taken down and may be used in evidence."

"Against me," added Reeves as if the phrase were not complete.

"No, sir. I said in evidence."

"But against who else could it be used?"

"That is not for me to say."

This was one of the cues for which Reeves had been waiting. "No," he declaimed. "It is not for you to say, but I know. I know that what I say could be used against me and against me alone. I am here to tell you. To tell you everything. Not of the death of Barry Foster but of exactly how I murdered him and why."

Hardwick sighed. "Just as you please. But I think you are very unwise." From the side of the room Matthews wriggled slightly on his seat. Just how provocative was Hardwick intending to be? At any rate the effect on Reeves was anything but a calming one. "Wise!" he exclaimed. "You will be so good, Inspector, as to credit me with a knowledge of what is or is not the wisest course for me to take in my own affairs."

"As you wish. May we begin at the beginning. Your name and address?"

Gradually, and with the assistance of a great deal of patience on the part of Hardwick and Matthews, the more ordinary preliminary details as to Reeves' address and occupation were extracted. Next, in a fashion whose orderliness must be ascribed more to Hardwick than to Reeves, the particulars of Reeves' relations with the Shergold Engineering Company and of Foster's relations with that company were described. In some detail Reeves emphasised the interference, the fussiness as he described it, of Foster. He started upon a tirade on the subject of civil servants and was headed off with difficulty. It was, as Hardwick put it, very possibly true, but it was not to the point. At once Reeves was up in arms. "Possibly true? Of course it is true. Everything that I am telling you is true."

"No doubt. Certainly I should not like to think that you were deliberately deceiving us in any matter. But if we could keep closely to the point? I am sure that there is much that you have to say—"

"A great deal."

"Very well then. You have explained to us that your dislike of Foster was entirely in his official capacity, or perhaps I should say in the way in which he personally carried out his official duties. Had you no other reason? Some private cause?"

There was a short pause while apparently Reeves considered the point. "I have," he suddenly said, "got the whole story of what has happened in my own mind. May I ask you to be so good as to let me tell it as I propose to? I shall tell it no other way."

"You had no other motive then?"

"Of course not. Please let me get on." Hardwick made a note, '*Motive insufficient. Probably lying about it.*' He sat back quietly and obviously was ready to listen. Fortunately he was not treated to a further discourse on the alleged shortcomings of the Civil Service.

"I decided therefore that I would murder Foster and let me tell you that when I decide to do a thing, I carry it out. I arranged my plans very carefully. In the first place Foster had once made a sneering remark on the subject of my left hand. Personally," and he showed the hand to Hardwick, "I am very proud of it. I came by it honourably" (again the remarks made by his former commanding officer passed through his mind and were brushed aside), "and I regard any disrespect paid to it as absolutely insulting."

"The remark made was…?" Hardwick prompted.

"It was more the manner — the general manner. I commented on it at the time to Miss Trent. She works for my company," he explained.

Hardwick made a note of the name. She might be worth seeing, but he was not going to jump to any conclusions on the subject. He never did. Through his mind though passed the thought that it was as well that every wounded man was not so sensitive on the subject of his disability as the man sitting opposite to him. *For that matter,* he thought, *it's a thousand pities that when there are masses and masses of good chaps who have been hurt and who make no song and dance about it whatever, one man should carry on like this. It may put people off doing what is right for the others and that would be an infernal shame.* Meanwhile he underlined Miss Trent's name on his pad and drew an imaginary and entirely erroneous picture of her. Then he pulled himself together. Reeves really was having a very bad effect on him! He obliterated the sketch and went on, "So you decided that you wished to murder him?"

"Today! This very afternoon!"

"Exactly. Now, could you be as precise as possible and give us the exact details? The times are especially important."

"And why may I ask? Are you actually proposing to check my statements?"

It was of course exactly what Hardwick proposed to do, but he could see that it would not be wise to admit it. Instead he leant forward and said, "I am sure that I can count on your full co-operation, but I am also sure that with your brains you can see that everything must be done in the proper way. In fact I think that you are the type of man who would insist on everything being done properly." He glared at Matthews who had suddenly shown a regrettable tendency to look surprised and pained from the word "co-operation" to the end of the remark.

But clumsy though the bait was, it had been swallowed. His audience was listening, and Reeves was in his element. "I shall of course insist, as you say, on all the proprieties being observed. Let me begin at the beginning then. I got up at about seven and reached the office before nine. I like to deal at once with the letters that have arrived. I answered those with which I was concerned and got on with the rest of my work."

"Your duties with the company are…?"

"I am the joint managing director. I have explained that to you already. Please do not interrupt. I spent a very busy morning, a very busy morning."

"I had understood that one of your causes of complaint with Foster was that he had caused the cessation of Government contracts. Were you therefore so very busy?"

Reeves glared. "I spent a very busy morning indeed," he repeated. "When the Government realises that business men have other things to do than to run around filling up their ridiculous forms, we shall get on better. I hardly stirred from my desk till well after twelve. Then I had a few words with the other managing director of the company — there were a few points that I wanted to tell him about. Purely business routine matters. I am sure that I need not worry you with those?"

"Quite." Hardwick put in since an answer seemed to be

expected. He could check up on them afterwards, if it appeared to be at all necessary.

The brevity of the answer pleased Reeves. At last he was getting this rather stupid little policeman interested. "There were many points and I think that the instructions that I gave Arthur Shergold must have rather overwhelmed him. Too much work does. Perhaps the long strain of the war. I really do not know. I have an idea, but I am not quite sure, that he suggested a drink. Oh, yes, that would be quite possible. There are the small remains of a few drinks that we got in when fire-watching had to be carried out. We keep them in the fire-watching room next to where I work. It is in a way set apart from the rest of the office. You can even go in and out separately. Shergold's office is next to mine."

"We can come back to the plan of the office later, if necessary. Did you take a drink together?"

"But it will *not* be necessary. What happened there cannot be of any interest. However, as you say we can let it go. As to your second question, I never drink at the office in the middle of the day." He seemed rather proud of it. Then suddenly a look of uncertainty came over his face. "At least — did I today? No, of course not. How absurd of me!" The doubt cleared from his face. "I am mixing it up with later. I had better things to do, I must remind you, Inspector, than drinking at the office. Besides I had got both to take a drink or two with my lunch — a very particular lunch — and I had got to keep a very clear head all the same. I was going to enjoy every minute of that lunch. I was going to watch Barry Foster stuffing himself, stuffing himself very full, and for the last time. I hoped that he was going to say all the things that would annoy me most. Nor did he disappoint me. I was confident that he would not do that. You could rely on Barry Foster if you had the brains to understand him."

"Having decided then not to take a drink at the office, you left there — when?"

"How should I remember the minute? About quarter to one I should say. I know that I had had a very busy morning and that I was tired. Anyhow I got to Oddenino's a little before half-past one. Foster was to meet me there, if I remember right." He seemed to nod and then suddenly stopped himself. "What on earth am I talking about? Of course I remember right. I met him in the bar outside Oddenino's, the one that looks on to the street you know. We had arranged that in case — in case I was delayed by anything. We had a drink there, a rum cocktail."

"One?"

"No, two. I always have two. We had them outside the dining room. Downstairs."

"You moved downstairs then when you met him."

"That's right. No, it is not. We moved into the Café Royal. A very good place Oddy's, but today I thought that I would lunch at the Café Royal. We lunched on the ground floor. I never think that much is gained by going upstairs. You just pay an increased house charge. That's all."

Hardwick again made a note. He had a rather different idea of the values given you in different rooms in the Café Royal, but it was only a guess as far as he was concerned, and it was of no importance. In any case he was too prudent to make any comment and so Reeves went on happily, "Foster started with the *pâté maison*. Very filling. But he had lots of that. And then, something. Venison, I think. It usually is that, or rather it's usually pigeon. But not today. Do you want me to describe that lunch in detail?" Hardwick assented and for the next quarter of an hour Matthews' pencil was kept busy since apparently every detail was required. It was even ascertained that the claret was a Mouton Rothschild '34.

"Thank you." Hardwick concluded at the end. "That is all very clear." To himself he admitted that it was almost too clear, or that at least it was too detailed and circumstantial. And yet — and yet, if one was just about to commit a very precisely planned murder, perhaps one would remember all the details most clearly. "You started lunch then, I think you said about half-past one?"

"Between half-past one and quarter to two, I should say. On the whole we did not take long. I should say that we left about quarter-past two. Then we went back by bus. I must tell you the best joke though, Inspector. Not only did I make Foster go back by bus when he was hoping for a taxi, but I made him pay for the bus tickets! Fancy making a man pay for the bus fares to take back to his flat the man who was going to kill him in a few minutes' time. Damned funny, I call it. You should have seen him put those tickets into the ticket box when he got off! There was a 'protest' written all over his fat, smug face. If he had only known!"

"Yes, very entertaining no doubt." Hardwick did not sound amused, however. "That would be about…?"

"I should think we got there at about quarter to three. I carried out my purpose at about, I should say, three; got back to the office about quarter to four, had a few words with Shergold — say four-fifteen. I am just clearing off these tiresome questions of time, Inspector, since I think that they seem to worry you. Where was I? Oh yes. I had a few words with Arthur until, I suppose, quarter-past four. After that I had intended to go straight round to you. In fact, really, I am a little confused to think why I did not. It is the only thing which is not absolutely clear in my mind. So I had a rum cocktail and then felt very sleepy."

"You took a rum cocktail at four-fifteen on coming back?"

"Yes. A sort of celebration. No, what are you talking about? Of course I did not drink a cocktail at quarter-past four in the afternoon. Quite the wrong time of day to do any such thing. No, I finished my talk with Arthur and then — a very extraordinary thing it may appear to you, but I had been under, I suppose, a greater nervous strain than even I am accustomed to support. I felt sleepy! Extraordinary thing, you will agree?" Before the Inspector had the chance to reply Reeves answered himself. "But then I am a very remarkable man. How many other people would be able to give you so detailed an account? You will do me the justice to admit that I am calm and collected and not flustered in any way."

"Exactly so. But to finish the time question first. You felt a little sleepy at quarter-past four, you say?"

"Oh I put that aside. Chucked myself on what used to be the fire-watcher's bed, shut my eyes for a minute, blinked twice and was as fresh as a daisy. Then I came round here. I got here at quarter to five."

"A few minutes after." Hardwick looked at a paper on his desk.

"Why, yes." Reeves gave a smile. "To tell you the truth I actually hesitated when I got here. Somehow, I had an idea that I must do the thing in the right style and I hardly liked the look of the constable at the gate. A shifty sort of fellow to my mind. It will seem to you most peculiar, but do you know I walked down to just opposite the Houses of Parliament and I looked at Big Ben? There is something so very refreshing about Big Ben, I find. So complacent and certain of itself. One could not imagine it being wrong. It gave me confidence and I went straight back and talked to your constable. Not such a bad fellow perhaps after all, though a little impertinent. I think you ought to tell him to treat people in my position with more respect, more seriousness. After all one does not do this sort of thing every day."

Hardwick gasped and gravely said he would see to it and then returned to the point. "Very clear, if I may say so, your times are."

"Not a bit. Nothing is accurate to more than quarter of an hour."

"Perhaps. But I should not expect anything closer." Hardwick's face was grave and though Reeves looked at him with a faint suspicion that irony might be about, he could trace none. Hardwick went on gravely, "But in running through the times, we have left out other important details. Your conversation with Mr Shergold for instance. But really we had only got to the moment when you got off the bus and watched Foster put the tickets into the box."

"Yes. Putting those tickets back surprised me. I should have thought that as a civil servant he would have been wasteful of paper. Besides he was a wasteful kind of man."

"Quite. But the events afterwards? You have not told us about the murder yet, you know."

"Oh, the murder. Do you really want me to tell you about that?" Reeves' interest seemed to have languished.

* * *

FOR A MINUTE or two there was silence. Then the telephone rang. Before Hardwick had time to do more than to begin to mutter, "I told them to keep the telephone away—" Matthews took the call. His face was impassive as he listened, and he spoke as little as he could.

On the other end though was a large and rather angry doctor. "Is that the Inspector in charge of the case of this man who has been killed in a flat at Maida Vale?"

"Detective Sergeant Matthews speaking. I am helping the Inspector. Who are you?"

"This is Doctor Grantham. In a stupid moment I said I would do police work because my partner, poor old Jimmy Carpenter, who used to do it for you in this part of the world, got killed the other day by a V2 and doctors are in frightfully short supply. But let me tell you I have no intention of going on with it for a moment longer than I can help. You haul me out at any time of day. I admit that this is an easy time, but I still had the rest of my day's work to do and now because you are in a hurry, I have to drop it all and do what you want. And when I try to telephone you, all sorts of difficulties are put in my *way*. Apparently, you are so important that you cannot answer the phone. Even now I gather I have not got the big chief himself."

"Are you able to give us a detailed report yet?"

"No. Of course I am not. You know as well as I do that I am not allowed to touch the body until you come, at least so your constable says. But I thought that I ought to ring up to give you just a very general idea."

"Just a minute." Matthews handed a second earphone to Hardwick and whispered the word "Doctor." Then he got hold of his note book and sat down. "Carry on, if you would."

"The man is dead. You seemed to have some doubt about it. I suppose you want to know when he died?"

"Yes."

"Well, I can't tell you. Especially as I can only look at him from a distance, so to speak. I will make a guess and say between two and three; probably rather nearer two than three, but I can't be sure. In fact it is a pretty wild guess. Do you want reasons?"

"They can keep; we might in the end. But generally the point of importance is what you are prepared to say definitely to be a fact."

"Right. Briefly my reasons are concerned with the warmth of the body, the amount of rigor that has set in and so on. The room by the way was rather warm. Yes, I have been able to get close enough to tell that much, but there is no need for you to worry. Nothing is disturbed. Cause of death, I suppose you want?"

"Yes."

"Curiously enough, I am not prepared to say. I want a much longer examination before I can give you that and I just cannot do it now. Why not? Because, Sergeant, those likely to die have their claims on me as well as the dead. In other words I have patients and one at least I have got to get to. Apparently, the man was strangled. Certainly there are bruises on his throat, but they are not so distinct as I should have expected them to be. I want a further and careful examination before I exclude other possible causes. I can manage a pm tonight and I want your leave to do it."

"It is not my leave that you want as you surely know. There has to be a pm of course but the coroner will give orders as to who is to make it. You had better get in touch with him. In fact you should do so."

"And if he wants me to do it?"

"That will be for him to decide, but if he does…" Matthews looked at Hardwick and, on his nod, said, "We have no objection, but not of course until we have been up there and seen everything that we want; photographs, fingerprints, so on. After that you can get on with it. The earlier the better after that."

"You're telling me. You had better have a telephone number where you can find me when you are ready and do look snappy." Matthews, annoyed that he had had at last to take so coherent a share in the conversation, as well as with the doctor's last remarks, looked cautiously at Reeves but the young man's mind was apparently far away, and he hardly seemed to be listening. All the same Matthews spoke quietly as he added, "We should be rather interested too in the contents of the stomach."

For a moment there was silence in the room. Then Hardwick leant towards Matthews and said quietly, "This is all wrong. We both ought to be up at this flat instead of listening to this chap. However having started it, I suppose we must get the statement finished. I must keep him to the point though."

"What are you whispering about?" Reeves suddenly broke in. "I am perfectly sure that it is a thing that you ought not to do. I never knew such a scandalous place in all my life. I can get absolutely no attention from you whatsoever."

Hardwick turned to Matthews. "Read out the last sentence made to us, would you please?"

Matthews looked at his note book. "Your last remark was, 'Oh, the murder. Do you want me to tell you about that?'"

"The answer," Hardwick said, "very definitely is 'Yes'."

"Ah! I thought that I should interest you in the end. As I told you he made a remark that finally settled any doubts that I might ever have had. I jumped up from the chair of the writing table where I had been sitting and I went behind that fat, loathsome, insinuating toad and with the thumb and finger of my left hand — and let me add that the use of my left hand gave me a very special feeling of satisfaction — I seized his windpipe with the first finger and thumb and then to make sure — doubly sure," Reeves was repeating the very words he had used to Shergold earlier in the day, "I brought my right hand into play too and I used it just to apply, shall we say, a little gentle pressure to my left hand. He did not struggle much. In fact I think that he was rather surprised." Reeves looked round with an air of triumph. He had completed his story just as he had intended to complete it.

But Inspector Hardwick failed to be impressed. "And then?" he asked.

"What do you mean, 'And then'?"

"You came away?"

"Would *you* have stayed there?"

"I am only asking you what you did."

"I thought that I had already dealt with the trivialities when we went into the question of the time when these events happened. Went into them with a most unnecessary insistence of detail to my mind. My accuracy seemed to impress you; you may remember. At least so you said. Personally it is the only part of the matter with which I am not wholly satisfied."

Satisfaction did not seem a proper sensation to Hardwick and he felt that his growing feeling of disgust was in danger of getting the better of him. "So you went back to the office, talked over the matter with your partner and then came along here?"

"Yes." Reeves seemed a little doubtful though. "I think that that is right."

"We can easily check that up with Mr Shergold."

Reeves banged his fist on the table. "Once more, Inspector, I must tell you clearly and I hope finally that this attitude of yours in insisting in checking up my statements, my perfectly clear and convincing statements, is an attitude which I will not put up with."

It was not a habit of Inspector Hardwick's to let his feelings get the better of him. For a moment or so he sat solid and impassive. Then he said, "I have not yet made up my mind on the matter—"

"The devil you have not!"

"—partly because I have not yet been to Maida Vale Mansions—"

"I give you that. But really I should not have thought these hesitations were called for!"

"—but I must certainly detain you for the present."

"Ah!" Reeves sneered. "At last we are beginning to see reason."

"Your statement will be typed; in due course it will be read over to you and if you still desire to do so, you are at liberty to sign it." Underneath his breath he added, "And after that, if I can possibly prove you innocent, I shall damn well do so."

A minute or two later Reeves had been taken away from his room and he was at liberty to turn to Matthews. "As you know perfectly well, one does not make up one's mind until one has more evidence than we have at present. As a general rule I mistrust confessions — and with good reason, but I must admit though that this man Reeves is up to a point convincing. But only up to a point. Of one thing though I am most perfectly certain and that is that the case is more completely topsy-turvy than it ought to be. I like my murders to start at the beginning with the corpse and go on to the end with the conviction. But when you start in the middle with the confession — well, all I can say is, that it's all wrong! One thing too is perfectly clear and that is that it is quite time that I went up to Maida Vale Mansions. You carry on here — and if you can catch that idiot of a doctor and find out whether, if the man did die by strangling, he thinks that it was done with the left hand, and with the kind of left hand that Reeves has got. If so, the case is beginning to get its legs underneath it. All the same I'll be damned if I take his impertinence lying down." The last remark was muttered to himself as the Inspector left his office.

* * *

MEANWHILE AT THE offices of the Shergold Engineering Company, Cynthia Trent was not taking things lying down either. She had seen nothing of Reeves since the middle of the day when he had left her part of the offices and gone, she had understood — at any rate it would be a normal thing for him to do — to that part which contained his and Shergold's rooms; and the old fire-watching room. Ever since Easter Sunday she had had very slight conscience trouble about him. He had clearly been annoyed about something and she had an uneasy feeling that if she had gone into it at the time fully, she might have been able to clear the whole thing up. But there it was. She had not and the very fact that there was something of the sort interfering with their normal friendly relations was making for constraint and the constraint was growing just because the situation was not normal.

There was nothing very special in Reeves not coming into her office during the afternoon. He very often did not. All the same she had a restless uneasy feeling all afternoon. *He was trying to be impressive all this morning,* she thought. *It never does suit him and as often as not it means that he is going to do something thoroughly stupid — or has just done it. I wonder if he is in his own room? I think — I think I shall go and find out and I even think that if he is not, I shall go and worry King Arthur.* She picked up some calculations to serve as an excuse and finding Guy's room empty, she went into that of Shergold. She did not like the look of him. He looked altogether too pleased with himself and the irreverent nickname that she had given him with no desire whatever of being kind, suited him all too well.

On her entrance though the look of satisfaction faded — she had perhaps imagined it all the time — to be succeeded by a look of annoyance. "Yes, Miss Trent? I have had rather a shock this afternoon and unless the matter is very urgent—"

"I was only looking for Mr Reeves."

"Mr Reeves will not be returning. Not this afternoon at any rate."

Cynthia hesitated. That Guy Reeves was capable of taking an afternoon off when he should not have done, she was perfectly well aware. Also that Shergold was capable of making it appear that he had when in fact he was absent on perfectly legitimate business. She put down the papers that she was carrying on a table and repeated, "'Not this afternoon at any rate.' I hardly understand."

"Very likely not, Miss Trent."

If there was one woman in the world who consistently failed to react to being snubbed as she should, it was Cynthia Trent. Her head was slightly on one side and her foot tapped very gently on the ground. "But I think I ought to understand."

"Really, Miss Trent. I for my part hardly understand what concern it can possibly be to you. A very serious matter has occurred to one of the two managing directors of the company. That however is not your business."

"But it is my business. And it's no good your trying to high hat me. In the first place, I earn my living here and though I am thoroughly nervous about the job ending on me, because I strongly suspect that the whole business is in a rotten state, I do still work here. In the second place I — I am a personal friend of Mr Reeves."

"The first matter can soon be put right by the simple method of terminating your engagement—"

"And a lot of fun you will have trying to find a successor to me with things as they are. Don't make a fool of yourself." Perhaps for the first time in her life she really approved of the way in which clerical staff had been ruthlessly called up for the Forces or the factory.

"If there were no other reason, I should find it necessary to dispense with the services of any employee of mine who disturbed me in my office for the purpose of calling me a fool."

"Oh don't be so ridiculous! Here are we squabbling like a couple of small children when all I want to know is what has happened to Guy" (the name slipped out accidentally. Between her and Shergold he had always been "Mr Reeves"). "What *has* happened to him?" she repeated after a pause as she got no answer.

"I repeat that this is no business of yours."

"But I tell you again that it is. Look, Mr Shergold, supposing you disappeared, and one was told that you 'might not be returning, not this afternoon at any rate,' and that 'a very serious matter had occurred' to you, do you think that quite a number of people in the company, even those who know you less well than I know Guy, would not regard it as their business?"

"Possibly they would. And precisely because it would be a matter of business. Mr Reeves — and by the way that is his name in the office, Miss Trent — was not concerned with the business of this office to the same extent that I am."

"That may be so. I know that you have elbowed him out of everything that you can. Nevertheless I should be interested to know what had happened even to you and I insist on knowing what has happened to him."

"Very well then. Since you insist, I will inform you. Mr Reeves has since he returned from the army taken a very strong attitude with regard to the profits of the company. He apparently thinks that they ought to have been more. He also apparently thinks that if they are not more, we ought to be extremely popular with those for whom we work, that is to say the Government, since our prices must have been low. My experience is that no one is ever really popular, for long anyhow, with a Government Department, but let that pass. Mr Reeves therefore was not satisfied. I fear that I have been sufficiently unfortunate at times to have incurred his displeasure, but at any rate he had the sense to realise that I was indispensable to him. He therefore switched his petulance to another recipient, namely Mr Foster—"

"Mr Foster!" Cynthia could not help exclaiming. There was a certain amount of truth in that. The scene in the bar at Shere came before her eyes, "Oh poor Guy," she thought, "I must have been treading on his toes terribly hard and it never came into my mind for a moment that he was sensitive about him."

"Yes. Mr Foster," Shergold went on solemnly, "I am not surprised that you started. For though Mr Reeves' dislike was mainly for business causes, there were, I understand — other causes."

"Don't be an ass. Go on."

"I must again request you to be more respectful. I really am quite unused to this behaviour. However it apparently is necessary that I should speak plainly. Mr Reeves accused Mr Foster first of all of having taken bribes from this firm — which of course he had not. Secondly of having given us a poor name with the Ministry with the consequence that we are, as you yourself hinted just now, without future contracts from them, whereas we had hoped to assist in the defeat of the Japanese.

Finally — and here perhaps I touch on a personal matter — he seemed to think that he had some further personal cause of dislike. Not wholly unconnected with yourself."

"Oh! How can you? What absolute rubbish! And yet only just now you were trying to say that this was nothing to do with me."

"I was trying to spare your feelings, Miss Trent."

"Fiddlesticks! I have never yet known you care a brass rag about anyone's feelings. But anyhow you have got to get off this 'not very good for little girls to know' perch and tell me. What *has* happened to Guy?"

There was a short pause while Shergold seemed to be considering what to say for the best. "I am afraid that this is going to be rather painful…"

"Get on."

"Mr Reeves left here about quarter to one. He met Mr Foster at Oddenino's at something like half-past one — apparently by arrangement. I fancy that he wished to discuss the company's affairs and I should have thought that he would have been better advised to carry out anything of the sort here and in my presence but let that pass."

"Get *on*."

"They returned to Mr Foster's flat, it appears. An even stranger proceeding to my mind. It also appears that some sort of quarrel took place there."

"Quarrel? What do you mean? And how do you know?"

"Mr Reeves returned here afterwards and made a short statement to me. He wanted to write it down, but, on my advice, he went round to Scotland Yard. I presume that by now he has made it verbally to them."

"A statement? What the hell do you mean, Mr Shergold? For goodness' sake talk plain English."

"I had hoped that I had expressed myself plainly and clearly as to a very distressing matter."

"A quarrel. Do you mean to say—?"

Shergold nodded. "I understand that Mr Foster is dead. At any rate Mr Reeves believes that he is. Of course," he added hopefully, "he *may* be wrong."

Cynthia sat down. "Dead!" she murmured. Then she got up again and put her face close to Shergold's. "And you let him go round and confess? In fact you positively encouraged him to do so?"

"I hardly see what else I could do. There was no chance of his escaping. I thought that it was best in his own interests—"

"His interests! A fat lot you cared for him or his interests, you — you—" It was too much for Cynthia. There was no word however impolite, that summed up her feelings adequately. It was almost an anti-climax, but, in the end, she relieved her feelings by giving the senior managing director of the Shergold Engineering Company a resounding slap on the face. Then, not looking where she was going, in floods of tears she went down the staircase that led not into the ordinary office but either to the yard at the side of the factory or into the street. Unconsciously she echoed the words of Inspector Hardwick, "And after that, if I can possibly prove him innocent, I shall damn well do so!"

Without knowing that she was making any progress in the matter, she took the first step towards settling it one way or the other. She sat down on an old packing case and put her head on another case that was standing on end till her fit of crying was ended. There she was found by Tommy Yabsley — a funny old boy Tommy, not always over-honest, but until recently one of the Shergold Engineering's night-shift. Until now life had treated him callously and he had responded by getting what he could out of life, especially in the form of cash, in whatever way came most readily. As to aiding beauty in distress or resolving the matter of the death of a civil servant, he had not ever expected to take part in such matters. As for beauty, he had no objection to it. On the whole he did object though to civil servants. In his opinion they behaved themselves as toffs and they were not really entitled to do so.

* * *

AT LENGTH INSPECTOR Hardwick arrived at Maida Vale Mansions, not a moment too soon in Constable Troughton's opinion. That junior member of the detective force was both hungry and thirsty and secretly he was all in favour of being allowed to go home. Moreover, though he was not particularly squeamish, he did not like the appearance of the late Barry Foster.

Nor really did Inspector Hardwick, but then perhaps the previous account that he had received of him (from Reeves) had not tended to predispose him in his favour. He found, as he had been told to expect, a fat bloated man, with rather dark hair but with that fresh colouring whose combination with dark hair was supposed in Victorian days to be suitable for the villain of the best melodramas. He was sitting exactly as Reeves had said in the armchair by the fireplace with his back to the window. He was seated rather forward in the chair, his knees forward and his feet drawn back in the position that a man might adopt if he was trying to raise himself from a sitting position, one hand had apparently been gripping the arm of the chair, the other was relaxed, giving Hardwick the impression that Foster had been trying to raise himself from the chair with one hand and protect himself with the other.

Just a minute though, Hardwick thought, *it's the right hand that's free. Oh yes. I think I see. Reeves says that he stood behind him and used the first finger and thumb of his left hand to strangle him but that he used his right hand to reinforce the left. Foster must have tried to pull up his right hand to pull Reeves' — if it was Reeves' — right hand away. Personally I think that I should have used both hands, one on each of my opponent's wrists, and not tried to get up. What happened though is clear. He failed to break the grip at his throat, gradually his head was pulled back, and finally there he was as he is now, his neck pulled out, stretched, I should imagine, and his face staring up at the ceiling.*

Quietly and in silence he moved round and examined the body from every angle. Look at it how he would, the position fitted in exactly with the description that Reeves had given him. Hardwick, fully aware that it was possible that because the idea had been put in his mind, he might force everything to agree with that idea, tried hard to think of any other solution. But try though he would, he could not find any that was more suitable.

In this connection the condition of the neck was obviously going to be of importance. Foster had not in life had an attractive neck, or indeed much neck at all, but in death it was at least fully visible. The Adam's apple was fairly well marked, but the central line of the throat was not particularly clear, Foster being a fat man. Standing in front of him, Hardwick looked at the bruises on the throat. They were not very clear but as he faced him there was a fairly long and heavy bruise to the right of the centre line. To the left of the centre was a similar bruise but not quite so heavy, below; almost straight in the middle of his throat, but if anything slightly to the right, were three lighter marks. Hardwick thought a minute. Then he tried to carry out experiments on himself and finally, this proving unsatisfactory, he put Troughton in another chair in the room and standing behind him, put his left hand on to his throat suddenly. As he had expected the constable immediately tried to get up and indeed partially succeeded in doing so. "No, sorry, stay where you are," Hardwick said. "I'm only trying an experiment."

"My fault, sir, I knew that really, but one reacts naturally."

"Quite. Not uninteresting that you did. You nearly managed to get up, but I wonder if you would have got so far if I had been pressing really hard — like that. Sorry," he added quickly as a faint "oy" came involuntarily from Troughton. "Now let me see. If I use only the finger and thumb of my left hand, the marks come — where?" He looked carefully at where on Troughton's throat he was exerting pressure and then he glanced again at the body slumped in the chair. Yes. He would not be satisfied until he had confirmation from whatever doctor the coroner appointed but so far as he could judge, if he used the exact part of his left hand which was all that Reeves had, the marks that he would make would be, approximately anyhow, in the positions in which Foster had bruises on his throat, the three lighter marks being those that were made by the knuckles of his clenched fingers in his case, and presumably in Reeves' by the ends of his fingers. He released a relieved Troughton and thanked him. "Now," he said, "photographers and fingerprint people please. I can do what investigation I want while that is going on. Then we can have the body taken to the mortuary and after that the flat need only be guarded by the uniform branch. I want to look at those papers on the desk though, so I want those freed first by the fingerprint people. Get on with it."

While the experts were carrying out their work, he gave one last look at Foster's throat. Those three light marks were worrying him. He found, rather to his annoyance, that he could not recall exactly how much was left of the broken fingers of Reeves' left hand. It was however a point on which he could easily satisfy himself later and he worried no more about it.

The next point, which was to worry him, though the fact was not immediately brought to his notice, came from the finger-print experts. All over the flat there were plenty of signs of Foster's occupation, particularly on the papers on the desk, but there were none of anybody else's. The only conclusion which Hardwick could reach was that whoever had murdered Foster had, so that his identity might not be revealed by fingerprints, carefully kept gloves on from the time when he had reached the flat, right up to the moment when he had left. There seemed to be something positively indecent in putting on gloves to strangle a man with your hands! It was worse than using bare hands, Hardwick thought, but there it was. That apparently was what had happened. He made a further note. "Is it possible," he wrote, "to tell whether the murderer wore gloves at the time that he did the murder?" Neither the chair nor the body had revealed any traces of a thread that might have been part of a glove, but that evidence was too negative to be regarded as in any way conclusive.

But, leaving that aside, the absence of the fingerprints of the murderer made no sense at all if it were Reeves, for Reeves had not, it would appear, ever intended to conceal the fact that the crime was his. On the contrary he had been anxious to tell the world. Why therefore should he wear gloves? Hardwick thought the point over. So far as he could see there could be only one explanation — that Reeves wished the whole of the evidence against himself to come from himself and from no other person or thing. It was in keeping with the egotistical character of the man, yet the careful evidence of fingerprints really seemed to be, in simple phraseology, overacting. And in Hardwick's experience common sense was a good guide. A thing which made no sense at all usually required some further explanation. It might be there, but it had to be found.

The papers however, at first sight, were uninteresting. It was true that they were concerned with the Shergold Engineering Company, but they were only dry, official documents, containing a report on the actual costs of various contracts and sub-contracts which had been carried out by the Company. They were about as exciting as such figures usually would be — that is to anyone not directly concerned. In addition, open beside the table, was a black bag of the familiar Government pattern with which civil servants are provided to carry about papers, a stout serviceable article of a standard pattern. In it were various instructions to Foster from his department to the effect that he was to visit certain companies and find out certain information, there was a report or two of Foster's returned for correction (with some acid comments from Foster attached), there was a folder containing loose stationery at the back of which it appeared Foster had been in the habit of keeping his claim for travelling expenses and the weekly time sheet on which he recorded his movements. Finally — an enormous and bulky packet — were the instructions of the department as to how in general investigations were to be carried out, an enormous and varied mass of words.

Putting aside the other papers for later examination, if necessary, Hardwick turned to the records of Foster's own movements. It appeared to have been his practice to use his time sheet as a kind of diary. The names of the companies that he proposed to visit were recorded throughout the whole of that week, up to the following Saturday, April 21st. That day apparently was to be spent at the office. For the next four weeks his time sheets had been started and on them appointments had been booked, leaving blank only the hours spent on travelling and investigation. Hardwick turned back to the current week. He was amused to notice that the whole day had been allotted to the Shergold Engineering Company and that Foster claimed that he had left their offices a few hours after he was in fact dead. Moreover he had already entered his claim for his fares to their office, to which in fact he had not been on that day. *But there*, thought Hardwick, *his expense claim is nothing to that of some business people nor his time sheet to that of some workmen and I suppose that if a company insists on visiting you, they have mucked up your whole day anyhow and you have to put everything down as if you had been to them to make it appear realistic. There are times when over-checking just forces people into mild dishonesty — and anyhow I am not here to see if Foster claimed a few coppers to which he was not entitled. Besides, there was apparently that bus fare for two. And by the way the bus conductors and conductresses on that route had better* be talked to in case they remember it. *It sounds as if Foster had made a little scene and that might have fixed it in their minds.*

* * *

IN THE QUIET seclusion of Scotland Yard, Reeves was turning over in his mind the letter which he had written the night before and which he had posted to Cynthia Trent earlier in the day. It had been, he thought, a good letter and he liked bringing back the phrases of it to his memory. He knew it almost by heart.

"My dear Cynthia," he had begun, "by the time that this reaches you, you will have heard that Barry Foster has met a death which he has most amply deserved.

"You, who have known him longer than I have, will, I am sure, agree that a man who thinks that he is always right is at the best an insufferable bore and at the worst — well, what can be worse than an insufferable bore? Of course I know that you, out of the goodness of your heart, used to pretend that you found something in him that was of some use to the world, some alleviation to his utter dreariness, but that, I repeat, was only your kindness. No one else discovered these alleged virtues.

"Let us consider carefully his conduct. There is no need for me to go into his behaviour to the Company for which we both work. That must be known better to you than to me. Still, lest there should be any misunderstanding on the point..."

Of course after that he had gone over all the details with rather wearisome iteration, for no man or woman has ever yet said that "there was no need to go into" some question or other without going into it at length. With that off his chest, having narrowly missed being himself an "insufferable bore," he had glanced very lightly and by implication at Foster's relations with Cynthia herself. It had not been an easy thing to write about tactfully because, apart from anything else, even Reeves himself was not quite sure that there were any anyhow. He flattered himself that he had worded his veiled allusions so carefully that if there was anything, however faint, Cynthia would see what he meant, whereas if there was nothing, or that she thought there was nothing, she would not even realise that anything was being suggested. It was a substantial piece of self-flattery, but Reeves was an adept at deceiving himself.

"Therefore," he went on, "I came to the very correct conclusion that he was not fit to live and by the time you read this you will have heard that I have been round to Scotland Yard — or possibly I shall have written to them; I am not sure which course I shall take — and I shall have convinced them that I have murdered — how does one spell that word? — Barry Foster. It will be a very detailed confession because Scotland Yard are not easy people to convince. They have, I understand, a prejudice against people who confess to crimes. It arises, I believe, solely from professional jealousy. They like to find out things for themselves and anything which they are told, they think cannot be true, simply because they have not found it out for themselves. The natural suspicion, I suppose, of minds warped by constant association with crime.

"It will therefore be a mental exercise of some interest to watch their reactions, to observe the incredulity being banished from their faces and replaced by an admiring, though reluctant, belief. That will be the first stage and I think that you will agree with me that nobody could carry through such a feat in a manner so praiseworthy as I shall do. You have probably realised by now that I have abilities of a sort. In fact I have thought at times that you shrank from me because of their very obvious existence but let that pass.

"It occurs to me though that I have left you long enough in suspense. You will possibly be anxious about me."

When she had received the letter and read so far, Cynthia put the paper down. The sentence had been most carefully arranged to come at the foot of a page. Despite her desire to read quickly to the end, she had got to get her feelings right. The letter seemed likely to be such a maze of contradictions that she felt that if she were not clear in her own mind as to her own attitude, she would never succeed in understanding what Guy really meant.

To suggest that he was in the slightest degree concerned in keeping her in suspense for a few paragraphs when he had left her in suspense all night was ridiculous. "You will possibly be anxious" was also an obvious understatement deliberately made in the hopes of making her say to herself — very much more. Exactly what that more might comprise was the first thing that she had to settle with herself. *Of course Guy — he would — had obviously decided that if I have not fallen for him hopelessly head over ears before, this incident is bound to settle it. By all the rules of romance — and Guy is incurably romantic, anyhow in the sense that he dramatises himself day in, day out — I ought to rush to Scotland Yard and throw myself frantically round his neck. Or rather I ought to try to and find that it was impossible to do it there. When he wrote this, he probably imagined himself in the condemned cell singing snatches from the Beggar's Opera. Yes, I think he has probably conjured up some very attractive and extremely melodramatic scenes. I even wonder if that was the object of all this.*

Finding that her thoughts were running away with her to the extent of bringing a smile to her face, she lit a cigarette and resumed her thoughts. *Perhaps I am being rather a beast. I ought not to be laughing at him anyhow. Whatever he may have intended it is no laughing at matter for him now. For one thing that man is dead. Obviously, one has got to do what one can for Guy now. But all the same am I as much in love with him as he thinks? or at all? I must put aside his silly insinuations about Barry Foster. The insinuations are clumsy and annoying and hopelessly beside the point, so let's forget that. My good girl,* she addressed herself sternly. *Make up your mind. Are you or are you not?* For a full minute she sat smoking and thinking. Then she answered herself. *No. Not really. At least I don't think so. Or at all?* she insisted to herself, but she could only reply with a hopeless shrug of her shoulders. It was an answer that was neither helpful nor convincing even to herself, but at least she was determined to pretend that it was. She turned back to the letter and re-read the paragraph beginning "Therefore I came to the very correct conclusion." It was in one way a tiresome paragraph for though he might, as he said, have convinced Scotland Yard of his guilt, in his letter he neither really affirmed nor denied it. *On the whole though,* thought Cynthia, *I think that that is a good sign. In the mood that he was when he wrote this, that he does not absolutely insist on saying that he did it, is as much as I can hope. But let's get on.* She stubbed out her cigarette and turned over the page. It was almost impossible to resist a frown at the care with which Guy had arranged that his talk of "suspense" should necessitate at least the break required to turn the sheet over.

"But you will know me well enough to be sure that your anxiety will be unnecessary — provided that is that I am not so unfortunate as to come up against a really stupid detective. Personally I have the very highest regard for the intelligence of Scotland Yard, and I am quite certain that they will be clever enough, perhaps I should content myself with saying diligent enough, to find out that the story which I have told them, and which will rest wholly on my word, will be inaccurate in its details. After that the case against me will break down, especially if they have been foolish enough to charge me with Foster's murder, and for very fear of making fools of themselves they will withdraw the case — or whatever the correct phrase is. You see the chief evidence that they will have is my own confession and *it will be wrong in the details.*

"In the first place I shall start by describing a very elaborate lunch that I gave Foster at the Café Royal. I shall describe the scene in that dining room on the ground floor in some detail, the big square room and the red plush on the settees that are so well known to so many people. I shall mention a claret that you can in fact get there and I shall lay emphasis on the *pâté maison* which is a speciality there and very good too.

"But I shall not in fact take Foster to lunch at the Café Royal. I shall take him to Oddy's. We shall have a very nice lunch there, but it will be of a different kind. If the police ever come to know what in fact he ate for lunch," (Cynthia stopped for a minute and then realising exactly what he meant, felt a slight feeling of nausea. Post mortem on the contents of people's stomachs had always seemed to her peculiarly revolting), "they will find that it does not agree with my account. They will — I am relying you see on their skill — make exhaustive enquiries at the Café Royal and they will fail to find any trace of our being there. That will puzzle them. It is not easy to be sure whether they will trace us to Oddenino's. They may do. If they do, it will be a further puzzle to them to know exactly why I should have described in such detail something which did not happen. They will start — after they have, I hope, charged me — to get suspicious as to whether my confession is bona fide. Being the police and finding a fact that does not fit, they will try to invent other theories. They will in fact be prepared to believe everything except that which I have told them.

"Of course it will not be sufficient to rely on one error. They might not find the flaw — and it would be unfortunate if a well thought out plan should go wrong because of a failure on the part of the police to follow up a clue properly — and so I shall also give them a few other trifles. They will find themselves in a muddle about time, for I shall be a little inaccurate in my timing and I hope that they will spot this. If not, I shall have to hint it to them. But in any case, from what I have read," (*"Read." Exactly!* thought Cynthia), "of other murders, the time gets into a muddle more often than not. Again I shall make rather a point of Foster having to pay some bus fares. But have you ever known me go by bus? Of course I shall take a taxi — for the further confusion of the timing programme.

"But I seem to hear you say, 'one cannot always get a taxi when one wants one. Supposing you find that one cannot be got?' My dear Cynthia, have you ever known me fail to get one when I want one? I have even thought of abandoning engineering and offering to hire out my services to the American army as an instructor in the gentle art of taxi-catching. But, on the whole, I prefer the harder task of pulling the Shergold Engineering Company round, which you may be interested to know that I propose doing, Shergold or no Shergold.

"So there will be the second error that the police will find. Next, you know the passion of Scotland Yard for fingerprints. I shall not oblige them by letting them find any in Foster's flat. With me," (Cynthia rather shudderingly could imagine him stretching out his left hand and admiring it), "fingerprints would be so very decisive. But their very absence will puzzle Scotland Yard. Why should a man take the trouble to hide his participation in a murder to which he has already confessed? I can see my Inspector — I wonder what he will be like? I hope he is large and efficient in a rather routine way, or else an interesting person full of character and replete with eccentricities — turning that point over and over in his mind Finally he will decide that, whatever may be his opinion in the matter, he has no proof; that such proof as he has was destroyed by the credulity with which he has swallowed my confession. That the credulity was unwilling will make the destruction if anything all the more complete.

"You will therefore I think readily agree with me that there is no need for you to have any anxiety. I shall keep a clear brain. With anyone else, I agree that it might not be unreasonable to be a little apprehensive. But you can rely on me.

"There remains a final point. Are you to produce this letter? That is a difficult point and one which I shall to some extent leave to your judgment. You will, I am sure, readily understand that in doing so, I am paying your discretion the biggest compliment that I can.

"If possible, try to get to see the Inspector and form an opinion of him before you make up your mind. He will no doubt come to the office and you should have no difficulty in having some conversation with him. On your appraisement of him depends your future action. If you think him intelligent and likely to act the way that I intend him to act, there will be no need for you to produce this. It is only if he does not seem to be up to his job that it will be necessary that you shall come forward with it.

"Keep it therefore for such an emergency.

"You will have to use a little tact in producing it, if you have to, as your reason for so doing is, I am afraid, unavoidably made all too clear, but you can no doubt explain that away. You will have some explanation no doubt on the lines that you were anxious only to produce evidence favourable to me and you thought that this was unfavourable and that as you knew that I had confessed, you did not see that you could help the police, especially as probably by the time that you get this they will have completed their examination of my movements; they may even be on the verge of releasing me. Or you can develop conscience trouble.

"There is much more that I could say, my dear Cynthia, but there is one chance in a thousand that you may have to produce this letter and the remaining things that I should like to write are not those which should run any risk whatever of being put in front of Scotland Yard. So I will leave them unwritten — for the moment. I shall hope soon though to say them all to you.

"I know that I can rely on you."

Cynthia Trent put the letter slowly back into its envelope and so into her handbag. It was not a very convenient document to carry about or to leave anywhere. Supposing for instance that she or her flat were searched? She had no idea if such a thing were legal, but it might be. *How like Guy,* she thought, *to land me with a document that one hates to keep but cannot possibly destroy, which can safely be put nowhere, which I have no idea if I ought to produce or keep to myself, but whose production has carefully been arranged to be a most ingenious insult to the man to whom it is produced. Finally Guy must needs see to it that any excuse that I might possibly use to cover that insult up, has been most firmly given away. It does make things easier! In fact considering my parting from King Arthur last night, the position poor Guy is in, the probability that the police are all over the office, and finally what Tommy Yabsley told me yesterday evening, I am looking forward to today like hell.*

* * *

But for Inspector Hardwick the next day had not yet been reached. Some preliminary remarks on the medical side must be obtained before he could feel that he might take a pause. There were plenty of other things to be done but they could not be done that night. The medical side, though, could be touched upon. He phoned up Matthews and enquired as to the post mortem.

Matthews, it transpired, was not best pleased about the medical side. The death of Doctor Carpenter had been a very considerable nuisance for with Doctor Grantham he could not get on. Of course the decision as to who should do the post mortem lay with the coroner of the district in which the murder had happened and owing to a case which had recently been before the courts in which a doctor had carried out a succession of murders and avoided, for a while, their consequences by certifying them to be accidents by means of his own post mortems, coroners were inclined to use a different doctor to the one who had found the body.

Doctors however, to use a horrible current phrase, "were in

short supply," and finally Grantham had been told to get on with the work but not before he had discovered that the coroner had wanted to use anyone other than him and rather stupidly, he was a bit ruffled. His reaction took the form of being a bit slow. He kept on emphasising that he had much else to do and though this impressed, if saddened Matthews, on Hardwick it only had the effect of making him think that Grantham was trying to exaggerate his importance.

However at last Grantham had been induced to give what he was pleased to call a provisional preliminary report. Later he would produce a written one but since the police were so importunate in their desire for information, he would give them the main information to go on with.

"He seemed," Matthews told Hardwick, "to think that he was doing us a favour. When you consider that if Carpenter had been alive, we should have had the whole thing cut and dried..."

"I know; but give us what he has said. We can make other arrangements for future occasions. And we shall if I have any say in the matter."

"First of all he says that the cause of death was strangulation. At any rate there is no sign of anything else. Foster's heart was a bit poor, fatty degeneration or something..."

"Fatty — in war time?"

"Perhaps contractors took him out to lunch too often," Matthews suggested mildly. "However, he would not have died of heart failure unassisted. His heart did give way at the end and it may have prevented him from struggling but the cause of death was not his heart, though it contributed. Nor was he poisoned Grantham says. At any rate there is no sign of any poison. As to the contents of the stomach, it was not peculiarly full. That *pâté maison* that Reeves talked about so much would not show up specially, Grantham says, but he would have expected to see a bigger mass in the stomach than there was. In fact he thinks that Foster had had rather a light lunch. On the other hand the statement that he had had venison is apparently true."

"I see. I must talk to Grantham further, but it's about a fifty-fifty confirmation of what Reeves has said."

"About. But venison's pretty common anywhere. I asked Grantham about the wine by the way and he was only funny at my expense — at least he tried to be. He said that the claret would have left no trace behind and went on to be facetious about not being able to tell the vintage. He ended by adding that Foster had not swallowed the cork, so he could not tell me if it was Chateau bottled."

Hardwick grinned at the thought of Matthew's reactions to that series of remarks. "All right. That will do on that for the present anyhow. Go back to the strangulation."

"I was going to. Grantham seems to want to produce some surgical details, but I think that if the truth were known he is rusty in his anatomy and he wants to look it up in his text books before he writes his report."

"Blast the chap. Did you try to get it without the technical chatter?"

"I tried — of course," Matthews sounded pained, "but there was nothing doing. He did however commit himself to saying that the strangulation was done by the first finger and thumb of the left hand and from behind. He seemed to be fairly certain about that at one moment, yet there was some trace of hesitation the next. I think that that is where the anatomy comes in."

"I see," said Hardwick rather slowly. "But considering that he did not know what we have been told by Reeves…"

"Precisely. He is even inclined to be surprised at the force developed. That is why he looked at the heart. He did not suggest it himself and I did not want to put words into his mouth, but I am sure that if I had passed on Reeves' claim to have used the right hand as a reinforcement, he would have jumped at it. Apparently, a great deal of strength was required to pull the neck out in the way that it was. The man must almost have been pulled out of his seat and left hanging on Reeves' hand — if it was Reeves."

Once more, lingeringly, Hardwick murmured, "I see. All right. I will not say of this man Reeves that no doubt the man is a murderer. But if he is not, he is a precious good imitation. Venomous beast, too, Foster must have been."

PART III

"Oh, Sammy, Sammy, vy worn't there a alleybi."

— PICKWICK PAPERS.

Cynthia Trent put down Guy's letter with a sigh. It was all very well hoping to deceive the Inspector in that way, but surely it was far too naïve. Firmly, with a deliberate lack of logic, she put aside the possibility that Guy might after all have done it. After all, he did not actually say anywhere in the letter that he *had,* and she did not wish to think that he had, so she presumed that he had not. It was more convenient that way.

Nevertheless, if she had made up her mind on that subject, there were others on which she had not. In the forefront, simply because it had to be dealt with first, there was the question of her relations with the company. *Very likely,* she thought to herself, *that will be settled for me, since managing directors cannot like having their faces slapped by — what am I? a glorified comptometer operator and little more, I suppose, though I like to give myself fancy titles. Besides after what that man Yabsley told me last night, just exactly how do I go on? Oh, hell! Anyhow, first things first. I suppose I had better get to the office and get on with the things immediately in front of my nose and see how things develop. I cannot think though that I shall be very bright!* For that at least she might well be pardoned since the interview of the previous night had not helped her night's sleep nor the morning letter her peace of mind.

In the first half-hour at the office — and she had arrived late too for the first time in her life — she had achieved what should normally have taken her about ten minutes. It was almost a relief when she received the expected summons to go to Mr Shergold's office and be interviewed by "King Arthur."

"Ah! Miss Trent, yes. Ah, good morning. Sit down, if you please." Shergold did not seem to be at all at his ease. As she sat down it passed through her mind to murmur that he would be safer thus, at least his face was safe. It would, however, have been a tactless remark at the best of times and on this particular morning she made up her mind to say as little as possible.

"You have seen this morning's paper?" Shergold, toying with a pencil, was at last obliged to open the conversation. He did not seem to find her monosyllabic negative helpful. As however she vouchsafed no more, he had to go on. "Those that I have seen make little reference to the matter which concerns us so deeply. A brief reference to the fact that a civil servant has been found dead and that Scotland Yard have taken a statement from a man about sums the whole thing up."

"Newspapers are short of space these days."

"Yes, yes. Quite so. Somehow, I hardly regarded Foster as a civil servant. Just a representative of the Ministry who worked for us—" He twisted round in his finger the rejected component that lay on his desk.

"*For* us?" Cynthia had in mind various rumours in which she had heard it faintly suggested that Foster had been far too much "for" the Shergold Engineering Company.

"Well, perhaps I should say 'with' us. One could hardly say 'for' could I? In fact I fancy, and you yourself have been in a very good position to judge of this, that he has done us a great deal of harm with the Ministry but let that pass."

There was an awkward silence while Shergold appeared to be hoping that Cynthia would help him out, but as she remained silent, he had in the end to go on himself. "About last night," he began.

"Yes?"

"I wonder if you feel inclined to offer me an apology? I wish, considering your services with us, to view the matter in the most lenient light possible." Cynthia said nothing. She had begun to see which way things were likely to go and so she again forced Shergold to continue, "I can quite of course understand that you were overwrought last night, all the same I really feel that I ought to insist…" Silence. Irritating though it was to have the worst of a monologue, he tried again. "I had imagined that you would be anxious in your own interests—" Shergold stopped abruptly. He had remembered that it was the suggestion that he was looking after Reeves' interests that had finally caused his face to be slapped the evening before. Rather tamely he substituted: "For your own reputation to…to…It seems hardly a matter which one could explain to the Ministry of Labour. After all so…so undignified. I should be…more than ready…to meet you at least half-way."

"The Ministry of Labour!" Cynthia exclaimed.

"If I had to lose your valuable assistance, I should have to explain to them…I could hardly, after the requests I have made to them to retain your services, allege that I had no work for you or that you were doing it badly. Besides, with Mr Reeves, shall we say, away — Oh, temporarily. I am quite sure temporarily — it would be inconvenient — you can see for yourself that there is extra work to be covered. I should not be surprised either if the Ministry…" He trailed off into incoherence and sat watching her.

It was all perfectly clear to Cynthia now. The Company would find difficulty at the time in doing without her, but what was more to the point if she refused to resign and help them with the Ministry of Labour by insisting on her resignation, they would have difficulty in explaining to the Labour office why they were parting with her. Even if she did resign it would probably have to be explained, but if she did not — well, "Insubordination," she supposed might sound all right in general, but the details, especially those of the smacking of the Managing Director's face, would not be dignified and the fact, at present unknown in the office, she would certainly let out if she needed to do so. Cynthia was quite woman enough to be prepared to use a little gentle blackmail if it was really imperative. Nor, it occurred to her, would Shergold stand up to the fact that he had begun the original interview by insinuations which might be regarded as insulting.

"I hardly see why I should apologise," she remarked almost cheerfully.

"I should have thought that your final gesture — still I realise the difficult situation, the shock to your nerves. I shall consider the matter further before taking any action. Perhaps you will be so good as to think it over too. A night's sleep—"

"—Was not a thing I had last night." She made up her mind quickly to make use of the chance remark since there were several things that she wished to do that day which could not be done inside the offices of the company. Accordingly she went on. "At any rate I do not think that it is in any way possible for me to do my day's work today and so, with your permission, I propose to return home."

"Quite, quite. A day's sick leave. Always anxious to help an old employee and," he leaned forward and for the first time seemed anxious to impress her, "you will recollect that the company has invariably been a very good employer to you."

Cynthia thought a minute. "So you think that the police will want to talk to me?" she asked brightly.

"The police! Really, Miss Trent! A very unworthy remark.

You are clearly not yourself today. If the police ask for you today I will explain the matter to them. When you have recovered yourself, I think that you will do us the justice to realise that we have always behaved as an employer should. Setting myself aside, you might do Mr Reeves that justice."

At heart Cynthia was a fair-minded person. Somewhat abruptly, and in answer more to her own thoughts than to what Shergold had said, she answered, "That's just what makes it so hard. Because you have treated me and the rest of the office staff well. Even before G — Mr Reeves came back."

"Thank you, Miss Trent. Now I am sure that you will think the other matter over, tomorrow morning — or perhaps the day after…" It was quite clear that his chief idea was to get rid of her for the present without completely losing control of her and ruining the discipline of the office staff. As it was her wish too that she should get away from him for the day, at least, she went quickly. No doubt, she thought, later he will salve his pride by saying that he got through a difficult interview with great tact and finally contented himself by obtaining an expression of gratitude from me. He will instance that as an example of his moderation. She collected her things together from the desk and prepared to go. From what she could see of the office, not much work was going to be done for the Company that day. The staff were standing in knots talking. On her approach their voices would drop to a whisper. Thank goodness she had had the sense to arrange to get away for the day. It might cause them to talk more but at least she would be spared listening to it.

With her mind still not made up, she walked along almost aimlessly, but eventually her course became clearer to her. Stopping at a telephone box she rang up the Ministry and asked to be put through to Foster's extension. She was, she explained, anxious to talk to the head of Mr Foster's department. A voice politely explained that Mr Foster was not there, a remarkable understatement and then a delay, rather maddening to her, occurred while she was transferred from one extension to another. Eventually a suave voice informed her that Mr Pennington was out at the moment. Could a message be taken?

Cynthia felt her courage oozing. To pass on what Yabsley had told her was a nasty thing to have to do. It would certainly cause trouble to the Company and to Shergold — which worried her little — but it would also cause trouble to Guy Reeves and that she disliked very much. Yet she felt sure that the Ministry would find out in the end, for she belonged to the small section of the population who regard Government Departments as liable to be omniscient, and if it was found out, it was better that she should be able to explain that it was all Shergold's fault and not at all that of Reeves. Public duty, private interests, the various personalities involved were all hopelessly muddled in her mind. "I don't know," she began hesitatingly, all her old doubts raced through her brain. "Perhaps it is of no importance."

"What was it in connection with?"

Here she decided was where Fate was stepping in. She would give the name of the company. If it seemed to raise interest in the mind of the unknown man on the other end of the line, she would go on. If not, she would refuse to give a name, say that she would ring up later and forget to do so. She did not remember, however, what she should have known, that the murder (for such they could see that it almost certainly was) of one of their colleagues was not an event that occurred every day and that some interest had been taken by everyone.

Everyone indeed knew, since it was customary for those visiting contractors to leave a note of the telephone number where they would be, where Foster had been and on the name of that Company being mentioned the Ministry was all attention. They were sure that Mr Pennington would be interested and would wish to see her. He would undoubtedly be back in the afternoon. Would she name a time in the day convenient to her — it would be best to make it fairly late in the afternoon in case Mr Pennington was delayed? Perhaps three-thirty would suit her? Or could they ring her?

Cynthia said that she was not on the telephone and received the suggestion that if she liked to ring up before she came round, she would be certain of not being disappointed. Would she give her name? No, she preferred to keep that till later, having in reality no desire to find the police there at the same time, as she had an awkward feeling that she might otherwise find them. Very well then, she would be most welcome. The extension number, if she rang up again, was one hundred and seventeen.

It had all been most polite, but Fate had clearly decided that she was to talk to the Ministry, and now that she had committed herself, she did not like it. All the same Guy was in danger — in much more danger than he seemed to think in his letter that he was. Exactly how she was going to help him by what she had to say, she had no idea, but she had an intuition that it would lead to something.

* * *

INSPECTOR HARDWICK on the other hand had started the morning in very good form. For such part of the night as had been left to him, he had slept well, the war news was good — a commonplace at the time — and there was work to do. Naturally he was cheerful.

It is — or was — a common belief that the best detectives look first for motives and having by deduction spotted their man, then prove that he did it. In fact the method adopted by Hardwick at any rate consisted of the more prosaic way of starting by finding out who had the opportunity, by his presence at a given time in a given area, to commit the murder. The first thing to do therefore was to establish Foster's movements on the day before and since at the critical time Reeves claimed to have been with him, the first thing was to investigate in detail the story that Reeves had told. There was the office end to be looked into, there might be some hope of proving Reeves' movements from the office to the Café Royal though the chance must be a poor one. There was the Café Royal itself — though a crowded place such as that might well miss him. Finally there was the journey back by bus. With the times limited it should of course be possible with the help of the LPTB to interview all the conductors and conductresses on duty on the route. At least it should be if the LPTB duty roster had continuity as it probably had. If there had been the kind of scene which Reeves had described, it might well be that it would be remembered. Bus conductors and conductresses were well used to scenes of course and it might have passed unnoticed. The conductor too might have been on the top deck. Still it might be worth trying. He rang up the LPTB himself to ask for their co-operation.

He got it and got it almost as a matter of course. Yet the LPTB sounded a little sad about it. There was, they explained, the usual spring trouble about the introduction of summer schedules and you never know whether a little thing like that might not start it off. Someone might say that they were being kept when they ought to be off duty and that they had little enough time off anyhow, a not wholly unjustifiable remark, the particular LPTB official agreed in confidence. Still, if Hardwick would come himself or send someone to the terminus, he could see each conductor and conductress in turn. They gave him the hours at which he could on that Thursday first get those who had been passing up Regent Street on the route in question between, should they say, two and three in the afternoon so as to be sure, but if the Inspector did not come himself would he be good enough to send someone equally lucid as to what he wanted and equally tactful? The Inspector would know what the Unions were. To himself Hardwick commented that at least he had learnt that that particular official of the LPTB was tactful with his "equally lucid." He agreed and turned over for a moment the problem of the subdivision of work.

In the end he decided that he would go to the Shergold Engineering Company himself; Matthews should take the lunch at the Café Royal in hand and that the LPTB — whatever they said — would have to be content with Troughton. But he would explain to Troughton very carefully what he was to do and what he was not. It would be simplest probably if he showed the conductors photographs of Foster and Reeves and saw if he got any reaction from any of them.

* * *

As Troughton made his way up to the Cricklewood garage, he looked again at the photographs with which Hardwick had provided him. The more he looked at them, the less he thought of them. Reeves of course had been easy. His rooms were full of snapshots of himself of a rather flattering nature and even if they were none of them of recent date, they were adequate. But Foster had been really hard. At first it had appeared that no one had wasted a piece of scarce film on him while the recent police photographs which showed him with his neck stretched backwards in the chair in his flat were not at all kind — nor were they suitable to show amongst others for identification purposes, for they would, to put it mildly, call attention to themselves. The solution had of course been simple. There was one on Foster's identity card and one on his office pass. In the former Foster had leant forward, his head sunk into his shoulders with the result that he appeared with three unflattering chins. He must have resented the resultant appearance and remembered it as the second was taken, for in it his head was thrown back so that he looked as if he had just received a knock-out blow on the point of his chin. It had not made him look any more attractive. Moreover being an integral part of his office pass it had had to be re-photographed to avoid showing other details. That again had not improved an appearance that was not prepossessing at the best of times. Troughton looked at it again and made the comment that the chap looked exactly like one of the Gestapo and was bound to be picked out on sight as a criminal. There would be no doubt, he thought, of what the bus conductors would make of it. That is, if the photograph as finally touched up was not so bad as to be unrecognisable.

Whether that was the reason or not, Troughton could not tell, but in fact the conductors and conductresses were able to make nothing of it whatever. As each of them finished his or her journey, he explained himself to them briefly. He was from Scotland Yard — he wanted their help. Had anybody resembling anybody shown in any of these photographs — he handed them a batch of a dozen or so — been on their bus on the previous afternoon? Each of them, man or woman, looked at them carefully. They were clearly anxious to be helpful and were not averse to the possible interest that might be added to a dull life by being mixed up with Scotland Yard. It was clear that they would like to know much more of what it was all about, but Troughton had of course to let their very natural curiosity go unsatisfied. Three conductresses made tentative recognition of someone depicted. In each case it was a different person to those in whom he was interested and as Troughton was well aware that they were people who were not in the least likely to have been about on the previous day, he failed to take any great interest, a fact which was without doubt noticed by the shrewd conductresses concerned. The final conductress of all showed most interest. She looked very hard at the picture of a flashy young man with fair hair, "I'm surprised at you, young man," she said, "walking about with the picture of my brother in your pocket and asking me if he was in my bus yesterday. Don't your bosses know who you've got inside? Six months 'ard, 'e got, only two months ago. You ought to be more careful whose photograph you show to 'oo." Troughton was sufficiently young to feel that it was a little awkward.

The slight contretemps threw him out of his stride. Still for a while he persevered, but by the time he got to those whose buses would have passed Piccadilly Circus not earlier than quarter-past three, he had lost his interest. There was nothing for him to do but to go back and tell Hardwick that he could find no trace of Foster and Reeves having been on the bus route in question. The information when he received it did not surprise the Inspector very much. It was a trivial incident and might easily have been overlooked. Still the fact remained, Reeves' story had not been confirmed.

Fortunately for Hardwick's peace of mind, Reeves did not know of that. He would have been very pleased.

* * *

FROM THE POINT of view of confirming Reeves' story, Matthews was having just as much trouble. In the account which he had given to the police, Reeves had stated that he had met Foster at Oddenino's and then moved on to the ground floor at the Café Royal. He had made a particular point of the ground floor and Matthews remembered having thought that it was rather out of character. A man like Reeves, to his mind, would have been certain to have gone to the most expensive part of any restaurant in which he was. But that was not the point. His object was to check up the story told, and he would confine himself to doing that.

It was immaterial at which of the two restaurants he started, and it was more by chance than anything else that he went first to the Café Royal. He soon found himself in the Manager's office being given every facility. Even though the morning was still young the management agreed with him that they had no desire that he should carry out any investigation in any part of the house where he might be seen or heard. As they arrived on duty the head waiter and a number of waiters were sent in to him and were shown a similar collection of photographs to those which Troughton was to use on the bus conductresses. The reaction was not wholly negative. Both the head waiter and one of the wine waiters picked out Reeves. He was, they said, a fairly frequent customer, rather particular and inclined to assume that he would be given better treatment than that to which he was really entitled. Still he was generous and appreciative provided that he got what he wanted. Matthews grunted. We could all be that, especially in these days, if we got our undue desires.

When, however, it came to the question of whether he had been there on the previous day, neither man was prepared to be so definite. To be sure of a negative is never an easy thing but so far as they could remember, they had not seen Reeves on the previous day. The reaction of both was independently the same; they could not be absolutely sure, but their strong impression was that Reeves had not lunched there on Wednesday, April 18th, 1945.

With a sigh Matthews had turned to the question of what had been drunk and eaten. "The man I am interested in has given a particular account of the lunch that he had. I should like to know if it is possible for him to have had it."

The head waiter was quite willing to help, "and in fact," he said, "nothing will be easier. I can get you yesterday's menu." He returned in a minute or two with the manager looking slightly worried. "Here it is," he said handing the card to him. We keep a card for reference. Also—" he looked appraisingly at Matthews, "we have to satisfy a good many regulations. Our books and records are quite open for your inspection."

"For my—?" Matthews looked a little surprised.

"Well, you say you come from Scotland Yard and in fact you do because you have proved it, but in my experience almost everyone who has been here during the last few years whatever question he has started by asking, has in the end turned out to be from the Ministry of Food. Some busybody makes some wild statement and I suppose that it has to be investigated. That's all right by us, but it does take up a lot of time."

"I can assure you that I am nothing to do with the Ministry of Food," Matthews answered. Apparently, he resented the suggestion as a slur.

"Well, please yourself. But it doesn't matter if you are, you know."

Matthews read. *Pâté maison* was on the list all right. So was venison under the title of "escalope de venison chasseur." He looked at the manager and casually touching Reeves' photograph said, "This gentleman speaks very highly of the *pâté maison*."

"Very likely. Many people do."

"He speaks of being able to get a great deal of it."

"Possibly. The reason is that—"

But Matthews cut short the explanations. "Oh, I am not suggesting that it is not perfectly all right that it can be got. I have told you already, I am not from the Ministry of Food." He turned again to the head waiter. "But did any of these people eat too much of it on occasion?"

"Lots of people make pigs of themselves here. It's not our fault." The photographs were again flicked through quickly. "The only one I remember seeing here was this one," he again pointed to Reeves. "This must be a pre-war one though because he has lost part of his left hand in the war and rather advances that as a reason for his having more meat — which I never could see. So far as this *pâté's* concerned, he takes an ordinary amount so far as I remember, but really it would be the junior waiter who would know that, not me. Shall I fetch one of them again?"

Matthews hesitated. "No. I don't think so. I should like to look at your wine list though." He glanced at it and decided that his ordinary expenses account would be thrown out of balance easily if he had to do much entertaining. But that would be so, he knew, if he drank wine anywhere at the time. Anyhow the vintage which Foster had mentioned was obtainable. He pointed to it and asked if it was possible to know if any had been served the day before in that particular part of the house. The manager turned to some books and papers on his desk. "Some was served at lunch yesterday, yes. Do you want to know how much?"

"Only how many were served on the ground floor."

"On the *ground* floor? The answer to that," the manager consulted the books again, "is easy. None. It is not a cheap wine, would not be even in peace time and the call for the more expensive wines comes more from the restaurant and grill than from here or the balcony. And of course dinner is the proper time for wine, all the same…" He sighed as if lamenting the lost niceties of diet.

Matthews broke in on his reverie. "You are quite sure that no bottle of that wine was served on this floor yesterday at lunch?"

"Absolutely certain."

"Thank you. I think that that is all I shall worry you about. For the present anyhow."

From the Café Royal to Oddenino's is not a long walk. It just gave Matthews time for the simple reflection, "If no Mouton Rothschild 1938 was served on that floor at lunch yesterday, either Reeves did not lunch there, or he did not give Foster that particular claret. And now for Oddy's."

For a while the situation there too had been very much the same. He was met with the same willing co-operation, but again on the ground floor there was no trace of the rum cocktails which Reeves and Foster had drunk before going, as Reeves had alleged, to the Café Royal. Though Matthews had started early the time was drawing near when the bar would be open and however politely he might disguise the fact, the bar cocktail-shaker was anxious to see the last of him. Had he tried the bar downstairs? It was at least an idea and Matthews decided, in fault of anything better, to follow it up.

To his surprise he met with some success. The barman picked out Foster from the atrocious and unkind photograph which was all that had been given to Matthews as well as to Troughton. Yes, that gentleman had been there on the day before. He remembered taking a particular dislike to him. An ugly, coarse, rather selfish face. He had been with someone else who had paid for the drinks and who had, when his companion was not looking, changed the glasses, so that this man (he tapped the photograph), had had the best part of four cocktails. He had noticed it and had imagined that it was some business deal and that it was desired to get the man in, should he say, "an easy frame of mind?" "If it had been earlier in the war, I should have looked a bit closer still, especially if it was someone in uniform whom someone might be wanting to get to talk, but as it was, I hardly noticed the gent who paid, except to notice that he was not wasting any excessive amount of money on me, whatever he did to the man with him."

"Did you notice where they went to lunch?"

"In the restaurant, I think. Not the brasserie. It's more classy in the restaurant."

"Would you know which table?"

"No, that I wouldn't, sir. None of my business."

"Quite. Could you put a time to it?"

"Well, not what you might call exactly. To tell you the truth I'm so busy that I hardly notice the time, except opening and closing time that is. But at a guess I should say about one, might be a bit before, rather that than a bit after."

"I see. Can you fix that on anything?"

"To tell you the truth, I can't. I can't even be sure that I'm right, but if I have to say something..."

"You would say that."

"Exactly."

"By the way — what sort of cocktails?"

"Rum. We call a spade a spade here and don't use fancy names to cover things up."

Matthews thanked him and turned his attention to the restaurant staff. Again he began the exhibition of his photographs. It would have hurt his feelings very much if he had known that the waiters referred to them behind his back as his "filthy postcards." At first, he did not have much luck with them but in the end a waiter was found who was fairly sure that he remembered Foster, though his identification was a little uncertain.

Once over that however he became more detailed. "One of the two of them suggested *pâté maison* but there wasn't any. We don't often serve it. We usually start those who want filling up with spaghetti. 'Spaghetti Bûcheronne' they call it. This chap seemed rather disappointed about it. Apparently, he had rather set his heart on letting his friend have some. So they had something else. I forget what, soup, I think or was it *hors d'oeuvres*? I wouldn't know. Then they both had venison. One of them seemed rather relieved that that was so, though why I have no idea. Venison is pretty common these days. In fact it seems to be one of the stand-bys."

"And to drink?"

"The one who was ordering asked for a bottle of claret — that really is why I remember the incident at all — and this one," he pointed to Foster's photograph, "looked surprised and pleased. Apparently, it was more than he had expected."

"I see. Do you happen to remember the vintage?"

"What vintage people get is not my business. In fact all I did was to call the wine waiter to him and tell the chap to order it from him. I have an idea that if people ask for claret, we have a particular wine which we serve to people who say that. Most people want the wine list and do a lot of choosing. Especially in these days when they want all the fun they can get for their money. Most of them want to see the price too. In fact I cannot remember anyone else for a long while just saying 'claret.'"

"Would there be any chance of his getting Chateau Mouton Rothschild 1934?"

"I keep on saying that it is no business of mine but if you ask my opinion, he wouldn't have a hope. That sounds as if it were something special."

Matthews hesitated. It did agree and yet it did not. The identification of Foster seemed to be fairly satisfactory but there was no identification of Reeves. "You remember this man," he said, pointing to Foster, "can't you tell me something of who was with him?"

The waiter tried for a minute and looked through the photographs again. To Matthews' mind he seemed to hesitate at that of Reeves. Then he passed it by and gave it up. "No," he said. "I just can't remember a thing about him. I couldn't even start to give you any sort or kind of description. I wish I could. I just happen — and it's the purest chance that I do happen — to remember this fellow's ugly face, something of the talk about food and the demand for the bottle of claret."

"Now I wonder why you should remember just that much?"

The man paused a bit and then said. "The mean dog. I think he sort of kept his face away from me while the other man didn't worry."

"Kept his face away? Why?"

"So that I shouldn't know him again. People who have lunch for two with a bottle of claret are right to keep their faces to themselves if all they're going to give you is a bob. No wonder he hurried the other chap off quick at the end without looking much at me. If I see him again and recognise him, I shall hope there won't be a seat for him — and if there is, everything will be off. The only thing that worries me is that I shan't recognise him."

"I see." Matthews did a little thinking. It was an odd way to mark the incident in the waiter's mind, but it had called attention to Foster — though it ought to have called attention to Reeves. On the other hand it might mean something quite different. He wondered what Hardwick would think of it. He was just about to send the waiter off, and indeed the man was half out of the door when he turned back. "I do just remember one thing about the other man," he said. "Now I come to think of it. I have an idea that he held his fork with two fingers, rather clumsily."

The sergeant turned round quickly, "With two fingers?"

"It might have been a finger and thumb. I don't remember very clearly. Something of that sort though."

Matthews had to exercise great restraint not to put words into the man's mouth, which he had an idea might all too easily be done. As a result, if he did not get anything that he ought not to have done, he did in fact get no more. The fork had been held in the left hand between two fingers or perhaps a finger and thumb and it had been held rather clumsily, a term which the waiter had been quite unable to elaborate or explain.

Naturally the wine waiter was the next to be interviewed, but he had nothing to say. He was, he explained, far too busy to notice the faces of people lunching there; besides there were so many. He flicked through the photographs a little more rapidly than Matthews felt was really respectful to the Yard and seemed to imply that Matthews was not paying due deference on his side to Oddenino's. He expatiated a little on their enormous clientele and he was clearly not going to recognise anyone. Not that he was in any way disobliging. In fact he went out of his way to fetch his records and confirmed that a bottle of claret had been served at the table in question or anyhow to one looked after by the waiter who had just gone out. Beyond that he could not go, except to say that there was no possible chance of its having been the vintage Matthews named. He mentioned something much more ordinary.

For the moment Matthews could get no further.

* * *

BACK IN HER flat Cynthia was thinking over what Yabsley had told her. She would have much preferred to have lain down and gone to sleep, but the lying down was all that she could accomplish, since the words in which she would tell her story to the Ministry that afternoon kept turning in her mind.

In a moment of panic she suddenly decided that Scotland Yard might want to see her, and she decided at once that she would very much rather they did not until she had got herself much more under control. Whether they had in fact heard of her or not she had no idea, but it would be as well to take precautions and for that reason to stay at home was impossible in case they looked for her there. She must get out at once and since she might as well kill two birds with one stone, she directed her footsteps so as to take her nearer to the Ministry. She might as well sit on a chair in the park as anywhere else. It would pass the time and it would be a sensible thing to get what air there was on a stuffy day, especially as she had a headache.

Even so the minutes passed slowly. She was far too worried to think of lunch and she was glad when, her appointment confirmed, she found herself talking to Mr Pennington. A quiet, nice rather fatherly man she found him and her opinion of him went up when after one look at her, he managed to get her a cup of tea. As she drank it, he kept her off the subject which she had come to see him about and made a few general remarks about the war. At length however he apparently decided that she had settled down and with a quiet, "So you work for Shergold Engineering?" he opened the subject.

"Yes." Now she was here she hardly knew how to start. Her careful rehearsed sentences all flew from her mind and to her surprise she heard herself saying, "I never did think their wages were right." It was not a subject on which she had really thought before but now that she had said it, she suddenly came to the conclusion that it was exactly what she did think and had always thought.

"Do you keep the wages book?" Pennington prompted. He would like to know how good her information was. Besides he found her a little hard to place and he wanted to gain time.

"No. The cashier does now but Mr Shergold used to do that himself at one time. Which is just what I thought was odd. It was too petty a job for him ever to have done really, especially as he never was the sort of man to do petty jobs. We call him 'King Arthur.'"

"I see. Arthur being his Christian name?"

"Yes. Of course there is no reason why he should not, but still — he just used to tell the cashier the amount of the cheque and the money was brought to him."

"The exact amount?"

"I — I think so. He used to make it up in packets and give the packets and a list to the work's foreman to pay out. The men signed that list."

"Was the list added up?"

"It used to have a pencil total at the bottom."

"Used to—?"

"Yes. Something worried him about it. I should think it was two years ago, but it might have been three. Anyhow just before Mr Foster started asking for the insurance cards."

"Was the system changed?"

"Not at once. In fact, it went on the same way until 'Pay As You Earn' came in. That system seemed to annoy him. I overheard him say that it made it too difficult, but I am rather doubtful if he meant me to hear that. After that the list was added up properly and the cashier did all the work. He grumbled a bit at having to do it when it became more complicated but then, as I told him, he might have had to do it all the time, which he had to admit was true."

There was a pause which was broken by Pennington asking her if that was what she wanted to come round to tell him. It hardly seemed to him that she would have thought it worthwhile unless she was more skilled in petty frauds than he thought she was, for the system that she described, though it might be all right — and should be if Foster had done his work properly — might not be quite watertight. He would have to follow up one or two ideas which came into his mind. Meanwhile his reverie was interrupted by Cynthia answering.

"No. It isn't. In fact I didn't really come round to talk about that at all. It just came into my mind though. I suppose it's being in a room like this."

"It's a pretty gloomy room, I agree," Pennington laughed, "but if you will tell me how to make files look attractive or figures interesting, I shall be moderately grateful. Only moderately, because by now, I am absolutely used to it. Completely in a rut, if you like. But what was it you came round to say?"

Faced with the direct question, Cynthia suddenly asked if she might smoke a cigarette.

"Heavens, yes. I'm sorry I didn't offer you one. Here you are." He produced a lighter and sat back expectantly.

"We have one part of the works which has always been kept a little hush-hush," Cynthia began. "It was making quite small parts and there was a sort of suggestion put about that they were terribly secret parts — Radar was the great idea, if I remember right, but nobody quite knew."

"There were drawings though?"

"There were drawings, but not supplied by you or any other department. Mr Shergold got them, and nobody knew where from. That was supposed to be part of the security. Another part was that no one knew where the parts went to. Once made they were collected, roughly packed, and taken to Mr Shergold. He took them away."

"How?"

"In his car. It was called the work's car, but I do not suppose that I have to tell you what that means."

Pennington shuffled uneasily. "How can we tell whether any particular car is or is not being used for the business? Or for that matter on which car the expense is incurred. We are absolutely bound to allow such things as an expense and hope that the petrol people will deal with any...nonsense. Of course there are the auditors too."

Cynthia nodded. She had always thought that it was easy to put a fast one over the Ministry. "That is about what I imagined. But anyhow there was no difficulty in Mr Shergold taking these parts away. Nor could anyone in the works definitely say it was wrong. An odd query rose now and then but there was always an answer. For that matter I rather fancy that there is an answer now."

"But now you yourself are sure that there is something wrong?"

"If Yabsley — he is, or perhaps I should say was, one of the night-shift — is to be believed. The only trouble though — and I think that it will save trouble if I tell you this in advance — is that you will never get him to say it. In the first place he would rather be shot than talk to a Government Department who are the sort of folks whom he does *not* like. Next to some extent he has to give other people on the night-shift away, people who worked with him. Of course they can all play the village idiot and pretend that they did not know but equally of course, they really did. You could never fasten anything on to them, but the other men in the factory wouldn't like it and would throw it in their teeth."

"I wonder," said Pennington. "I don't know what it was yet, but sometimes the sort of thing that I imagine that you are talking about is regarded as clever. Getting money out of the Government is always regarded as a fair game by some people."

"Of course it is. At least I don't mean you to imagine that I would — that I think that—"

Pennington smiled. "Never mind that. What exactly was happening?"

"Simply that these small parts were not for Radar at all. They were all sorts of things for ordinary commercial use, the body part of darts was one thing. The night-shift would be booking their time to one of your contracts but in fact they were making darts and other things, all things that are very easy to sell — what isn't in these days? — for cash."

"I see." Pennington thought a moment, "There's a catch or two in that though. First of all, all these jobs were not cost plus. Some were looked at technically."

"Yes. In some cases there was a lathe — I don't know much about these things…"

"Nor is it my line, but I have heard of a lathe." Pennington smiled and offered some more tea.

"Thank you. Well, when the test was being made the lathe was made to turn as slowly as possible and so each one of the real things they were making for you was rated to take a great many more minutes, two or three times the amount I gather, than it should. If it was a case of where it was hand not machine work, then Yabsley or one of his friends worked as slowly as he could. Even so I fancy that it was the cost, plus jobs that suffered most."

"And we cheerfully paid that cost, plus a profit," Pennington remarked grimly.

"Oh yes. Mr Foster was bound to tell you it was due. Just because the booking was wrong. It was down to the wrong job."

"And Yabsley and Co did not object?"

"Well, without exactly saying that it was a fact, Mr Shergold managed to hint that the job was so secret that it *had* to be booked wrongly and that not even your officials were to know. Whether the men believed it or not, I don't know, but of course Mr Shergold looked after them."

"Looked after them?"

"There were some very nice bonuses to be earned," Cynthia said drily. "Some people will shut their eyes to a lot for a nice piece-work bonus."

"And we paid!"

"Generally, yes. Of course if the contract became a fixed price one, sometimes the fixed price would not cover *all* the bonuses. That, I suppose, is how the Company never showed very much in the way of profits. They were all in Mr Shergold's pocket in cash."

"And Mr Reeves?"

"Oh, no. They couldn't go into Mr Reeves'. He wasn't doing the selling."

"But he might have been doing the sharing?"

"He wouldn't do such a thing! Besides he had not been back so very long."

"Very well then. We will leave Mr Reeves out of it."

Pennington was by no means sure that he would leave him out in the end, but he was very certain that it would be wise to do so now. The pleasant looking girl with the rather ordinary face was quite likely to stop altogether giving him information if he insisted on that point. He tried a fresh line. "Another snag," he said slowly, "is the material. If anything was made on a sufficient scale to make any serious difference, it would want material and practically everything is controlled."

Cynthia leant back in her chair and opened her eyes very

wide. "Well, I'm damned," she said. "Are you really as innocent as that?"

"I — I thought that that was true."

"But it's perfectly simple. All you say was that your wastage was higher than you thought. If you cut up a sheet wrong, it all becomes scrap — and no one can measure scrap. Then things can be machined wrong. And anyhow if you play your cards properly, you can often get the wrong quantity issued to start with, or even to get two issues for one job. We could always get an extra bit of metal of any sort, except the very scarce ones and you don't want them for making darts and so on, if we really wanted it. Of course bigger firms with a really good store-keeping system sometimes get a little bit in a muddle, especially if they have a too conscientious store-keeper and a ton or two of brass that ought not to be there, but people of our size are all right. Bless you, there was no trouble about material."

"I see." Pennington played for a moment with a pencil. "We shall have to take action."

"If by that you mean enquiries with a view to prosecution, let me tell you that you haven't a hope in hell. Yabsley and his like will have no more knowledge when it comes to questioning them of anything having gone wrong than of — of the winner of the Derby ten years hence. In fact they are more likely to know about that. You will find all of them looking like a blank wall and being one hundred per cent non-co-operative. Besides, with no contracts from you that game is over. In fact there is talk of the night-shift being directed elsewhere. I don't think that they will be any more ready to talk if they are. It wouldn't be a good start for them at a new place."

"And you yourself?"

"All I have told you is gossip which I shall not be able to prove. And consequently which I shall very likely deny having told you. I have an idea that if anyone at the Shergold Engineering knew that I had told you all this, I should probably be treated as an absolute and complete bit of dirt. The other girls there regard me as it is as being a bit stuck up and inclining to put on airs. I'm not batting, if I can help it. It's up to you to grub about and find out. After all you have powers to look at everything, and you have been given a lead."

"A nice job that will be — with everyone against us."

"Simply splendid. But I felt that I had to tell you."

"Yes." Pennington put the base and the point of his pencil alternately on his blotting pad. "Why did you tell us?"

"I've told you. This is something to do with Mr Shergold. The police have got hold of Mr Reeves because he *will* say that he has killed Mr Foster. So anything that one can say to call attention away from Guy — I mean Mr Reeves—"

"I see." In his opinion Cynthia had explained quite a lot. Without, however, commenting on that, he went on quietly. "But you know I shall not keep this from the police. And when I have told them what you have told me, I think that they will want to talk to me — and to you."

"Are the police investigating your Mr Foster's death or the cost of your contracts?"

"Foster's death of course, but I understand that the police are a very inquisitive body of men. I have an idea that anything connected with the Shergold Engineering Company will be of interest to them. I am quite sure that they will want to talk to you, as well as to me."

"But I don't want you to tell them."

"Come, come, Miss Trent, are you quite sure about that?" There was a pause while Pennington looked at her. "I have an idea — in fact it is practically what you said just now — that you would be glad for the police to know anything that will divert their attention from Mr Reeves. It seems a much more likely reason for your action than any care or attention for *our* interests. After all we are only a Government Department and, as you said, no one cares for us. Besides it is also quite true, as again you have said, that it will be difficult for us to prove any fraud against the Company and that very likely our best remedy is just not to give the Company any more contracts."

"Which is what you have done."

"Yes,"

Cynthia looked at Pennington a little more intensely. That "Yes" had been, perhaps by accident, said most significantly. "Do you mean you had some idea—?"

Pennington lied for the credit of the Ministry. "We are not perhaps quite so foolish as we pretend to be. Perhaps we could not have found out just exactly what was happening, but someone seems to have had some idea that everything was not quite well. At least, don't take that from me. It's only my guess."

"Then — perhaps — I may not have done Guy any harm?"

"By letting us know the way it was done? Well, perhaps if you can prove that your Mr Reeves was not really involved, who knows? It might even enable us to have a happier feeling about getting things from them — about future contracts. Only Mr Reeves just at the moment — and anyhow the decision would not be mine — besides we haven't proved anything either way yet. Oh, for heaven's sake, Miss Trent, do *not* look grateful. And — and don't do that!"

Pennington's deputy entered to find a young woman sobbing on to the shoulder of the head of the branch. "She seemed to be thanking him for something. No, I've no idea what," he explained later. "I made an appointment earlier in the day for her and apparently she had never seen him then, so I don't suppose it's a case of passing the hat around the office for wedding bells. You never can tell though. Downy old bird, Penny."

"How did he take it? Your butting in like that, I mean."

"Moderately well, but only moderately. He flapped a file at me as if I was a stray cat. I rather think he said 'shoo.'"

By the evening the story had considerably enlivened the small portion of the Ministry concerned.

* * *

INSPECTOR HARDWICK FOUND the offices of the Shergold Engineering Company without difficulty. He noticed their peculiar lay-out with only mild interest. It would, he saw, have been perfectly easy for Reeves to come and go as he pleased, but then it probably would not have been very difficult anyhow. On second thoughts though, while it might be easy for anyone in Reeves' position to take as long as he liked for lunch, it might not have been so easy for him to have done it unnoticed. That separate door did make the checking of the timing more difficult. It would also make it harder for anyone to produce an alibi, but at the same time it would make it reasonable that he should not be able to do so.

Mr Shergold was pleased to see him. In fact he seemed rather to imply that he had been expecting him before. There was something rather dominating about the way in which he greeted the Inspector. He would, he said, place himself entirely at the disposal of Scotland Yard "although, as no doubt you can imagine, I am pretty busy with Reeves being unable to look after his work. Naturally that falls on me too, but that I am quite used to, both after he came back and before. Besides one of my staff, a useful girl who has a considerable hand in preparing our costs, is being very temperamental about the whole matter" (he rubbed his cheek gently) "and I have had to give her the day off."

"I see. That may be a pity as I hardly know who I want to see yet."

"Really? That you would want to see many people never occurred to me. The story that Reeves told me was so circumstantial..."

"Might I have that story?"

"Certainly. He came back here yesterday afternoon about quarter to four and told me everything that had happened."

"He left here — when?"

"I should say a bit before one. But I don't really know."

"Did you see him leave?"

"No, I had gone out before him on a job of work that I had to do."

"Did anyone else see him or you?"

"Not as far as I know. You have seen our separate entrance?"

"Yes. But someone might have noticed one of you coming or going from it."

"Very possibly. I will make enquiries for you. Or would you prefer to do that yourself?"

Hardwick did not answer that directly — it was never his habit to state in advance what he would probably do. Besides the answer was obvious. Instead he asked what state of mind Reeves was in both when he left and when he returned. "Before he left?" Shergold repeated. "I noticed nothing very unusual. He was a little difficult perhaps. Something in our annual accounts for 1944 (they had just reached us) did not seem to please him, but then he was always inclined to think that the world was in league against him if everything did not go exactly according to his liking."

"And when he came back?"

"He was — how shall I put it? — exalted. He was full of what he had done, and he was going to tell the world. In fact he told you."

"Would you repeat what he said? It may be important. By the way I am having it taken down by the constable here."

"By all means. He said that he had met Foster at Oddenino's at about half-past one and that they had had a couple of rum cocktails each. I remember demurring at two because those cocktails are very strong, but he said that he *always* had two. Then they had lunch."

"At Oddenino's?"

"Yes."

"I should like to be quite sure about that."

"That was what he told me. He started to say Café Royal but then he corrected himself. He told me about the lunch in detail. *Pâté maison* for Foster. *Hors d'oeuvres* for himself. Venison for both of them and an ice. They shared a bottle of claret. He described to me how he kept on looking at Foster's throat as he ate. He even had a half impression that he asked what size collars Foster took, but I don't believe that he did really. It all sounded rather unpleasant to me. But there is was. He kept on, he said, staring fascinated at Foster gorging himself on *pâté maison*. Reeves always thought that there was something immoral in being fat and he kept on describing details to me about Foster's neck and chin. Rather unpleasant I found his descriptions to be."

"At any rate he describes things very vividly." In a queer way Inspector Hardwick felt that he was once more seeing the scene which Reeves had described but this time it was more vivid than when Reeves himself had been speaking. Perhaps it was the heat of the room, for every window was shut, most carefully. He looked at his notes. *"But I was not going to let him talk about food all the time...still I saw to it that he had his fair share of the claret... Please understand that I am not going to give you the lady's name."* He looked from the notes and saw Shergold looking at him very intently. "I have," he said, "a very full statement by Mr Reeves of what he said and thought. Could you give me as far as possible the words that Reeves used to you?"

"I think that I could. I was very much impressed by what he said — not unnaturally." Very carefully Shergold gave the conversation that he had had with Reeves, and which Reeves had memorised so painstakingly to give to Hardwick. Allowing for the natural interruptions that had occurred they were remarkably similar. "You have a very fine memory, sir, if I may say so. Very useful. And do you know who the lady was that he was referring to?"

"Do you think I ought to tell you that?"

"In a case of this kind I need hardly tell you that it is your duty to tell me everything."

"But really, I am sure that it can have nothing to do with the case."

"That is for me to decide. And if it does not, we shall not have to worry that lady much."

"Why shouldn't *he* tell you? It is not a nice thing for me to do."

"Was Foster's death a nice thing?"

"No. Not as Guy described it to me. Perhaps you are right. The lady was a Miss Trent. She works here. In fact she was the lady of whom I spoke just now as being a bit…temperamental."

"I see. I shall have to see her later then. Meanwhile you had got as far as the end of lunch."

"Yes. Then they went back to Foster's flat by a number sixty bus. Reeves made Foster pay for the tickets and he says that when they came to get off the bus, Foster made some little play with putting the tickets ostentatiously into the box by way of reminding him. A typical incident that. Foster, though perhaps one should not say such things about him now, was a very mean man. But let that pass. They got off that bus, crossed the road and went to Foster's flat."

"Quite. Reeves seemed to be a little uncertain of which floor it was on, but he thought it was on the third. Is that right?"

"I don't know. I rather forget the details of the inside of the flat as he described it to me, but you will have seen it for yourself. For that matter you will know which floor it is on."

"I forgot to notice. But no matter. Go on."

"Then there was some conversation. And then he killed him." In complete detail Shergold described exactly how Reeves had narrated his discussion of the Company's affairs and how finally he had given a description of his stealing behind the accountant. Once more Shergold's recollection of what Reeves had said was very accurate and once more Hardwick found a very clear picture presented to his eyes. He looked through the statement that Reeves had made. There was however one difference. "He led me to understand," he said, looking up from the statement, "that you were going to say that you were not concerned at all and were going to pretend that you knew nothing of it."

"I did say so at the time. And I am not concerned. But afterwards I thought that it was wiser to be honest about it. After all I could not go so far as to conceal his confession. Why should I?"

"I see. Now we have his movements. Might we have yours?"

"Mine?"

"Yes. Just as a formality. We ought to have everyone's, in case anything cropped up that we ought to look into. It would be easier if we have them now while they are fresh in your mind. I am sure you have no objection."

"None at all. Let me see. I was very busy all the morning — in fact the amount of work that I have left undone both by talking to Reeves yesterday afternoon and by the necessity of this interview is quite terrible to contemplate. However Government contracts are easing off now with the end of the war in sight and I suppose I can catch up."

"To go back to your movements. You left here — when?"

"I should say about quarter to one. I went to see a man in Elizabeth Street, near Victoria, to whom we sell scrap. I suppose you want his name and address?"

"If you please."

Shergold handed over a copy of a credit note for the sale of brass scrap. "That's a previous transaction," he said. "Yesterday I was only talking to him about price. He is not a very easy person to get hold of is Benson. Lunch time is about the only time that you can get him. He's got all sorts of interests. Anyhow I saw him about one."

"In Elizabeth Street. You moved a bit, didn't you?"

"Works car. It may be against petrol regulations, but it had to be done. Then I had some lunch."

"Where?"

"A restaurant just outside Victoria Station on the north side. I forget its name, but it has a snack bar downstairs, nothing on the ground floor and a restaurant on the first floor."

"Do you go there often?"

"Hardly ever. No one will recognise me if that is what you mean, Inspector." He permitted himself a slight grin. "But there I was from, I should say, quarter-past one — might have been later — until about two. I should think I got back here by half-past two. A long while before Reeves got back. That would give — let me see — half-past two to a quarter to four. An hour and a quarter. Yes, I should think that that was something like right."

"And all that time from 12.45 to 3.45 no one saw you?"

"Benson saw me in Elizabeth Street. In the restaurant of course lots of other people saw me, but I do not know if they noticed me. The same would be true here. When you check up on other people round the works, you may find someone who noticed me. On the other hand you may not. Don't blame me if you don't. But really, Inspector, you must excuse the question. Considering that Reeves has given a confession which so far as I know covers all the facts, why all this fuss and careful checking?"

Inspector Hardwick grinned quite unashamedly. "'You know my methods'," he quoted.

"I know what they are supposed to be. But in this case aren't you being a little, may I call it, stereotyped?"

"Call it anything you like but only amateurs and beginners (and not many of them) would fail to clear up all details. You have got to see first who was in a position to do the murder."

"Even if someone has told you that he did it?"

"Even then. He might be misinformed."

Shergold laughed outright. "I like the word 'misinformed'. It is hardly the thing that anyone would tell you about. Especially inaccurately."

"Nevertheless — Now, if you please, sir, I am going to leave two of my men here to take routine statements from everyone in the office—"

"And the works?"

"We will consider the works later. Probably just a general request for anyone who knows anything to state it will suffice there. You will give my men all the help they want?"

"Certainly."

"I should also like Miss Trent's home address."

"I expect we have that. I'll ring down to the office for you."

"While they are finding it, perhaps it would help if you will tell me the shortest way to Elizabeth Street."

"To find Benson at this time of day? Shall I ring up and tell him you are coming? I should hate you to waste your time."

* * *

INSPECTOR HARDWICK HAD RATHER DISLIKED the sarcasm of the final sentence, but there was no denying that it was true. Nor was he any more fond of the appearance of Mr Benson. He gave the impression that he had something to hide. Yes, he knew the Shergold Engineering Company Ltd. Yes, he had dealings with Mr Shergold. Not very frequent ones. He had bought scrap from them. Yes, he had seen Mr Shergold the day before. When? He had hardly noticed, but at a guess he would say just about one. What did he want the scrap for? Mr Benson became more obviously anxious than before to disappear without further conversation. Inspector Hardwick however stuck to his point. Mr Benson shifted his weight uneasily from one foot to the other and suddenly asked an unexpected question. "Is this anything to do with one of the Ministries?"

Hardwick countered with another question. It was never his habit to answer enquiries if he could avoid it. "Why should it be?"

"Well, I have an idea that it's their scrap. I don't think that it could possibly be of any use to them. I don't know of course if it is really, but I don't want to do anything wrong." It was painfully clear that he had something on his conscience and Hardwick pressed his previous point. "What do you use the scrap for?" he insisted.

Benson shuffled uneasily once more. "Darts," he said eventually. Despite the way in which it was said it did not sound very criminal to Hardwick. He returned to the question of the time that Shergold had visited Elizabeth Street, but it was clear that he was going to get no further.

Thoroughly dissatisfied he went away. Nor was he better pleased when he reached the flat where Cynthia Trent ought to have been but was not. It was time to have lunch — or rather as he soon discovered to his cost the time to have lunch was really over. Food seemed to have vanished from the town altogether. He went back and tried the restaurant where Shergold had lunched the day before, but he was too late there, or he might have killed two birds with one stone. He cursed himself for not having had the sense to go there at once. In the end he spent a considerable amount of time before he got some unsatisfying sandwiches of dry bread and rather peppery sausage meat. "In some ways," he thought to himself, "Foster was luckier yesterday. It gives me a pain in the neck to read over what those two ate and drank." He stopped suddenly. "A pain in the neck," was too literally true.

Rather crossly he went back to his office and received Matthews' account of his not wholly useless morning. Hardwick rubbed his chin thoughtfully. It did confirm, and it did not confirm what Reeves had said. He wondered what Troughton would find out, and, in his notes, he put down, *"Extend time. Try earlier."* Then he went at once to Foster's flat and read through the papers which Foster had been using in connection with the Shergold Engineering Company. So far as he could see they did not get him much further. Perhaps it would be useful to talk to the Ministry on the subject. He would fix that for the next morning. Meanwhile why the hell had he not got Doctor Grantham's detailed report? He took steps to see that he was put in touch with the Official of the Ministry who turned out subsequently to be Mr Pennington, and he also saw to it that Grantham was hurried up. "If necessary," he said to Matthews, "buy a book on anatomy yourself and teach it to him."

Then he sat down to think. Finally — perhaps it was the influence of Foster's half-finished report by the table beside him — he dotted down some disconnected though matured notes.

1. *He said,* he wrote, *that he lunched at the Café Royal. He described the Café Royal and the kind of meal you could get there. Including the right claret. But he did not lunch at the Café Royal, or at any rate Foster did not. Foster lunched at Oddenino's. And he drank that claret there that day.*
2. *Shergold says that Reeves told him that he lunched at Oddy's. He gives an exactly similar — and almost too similar — description of what happened at lunch and he gives the same meal. But Reeves apparently cannot have eaten that meal.*
3. *The bus. Not yet proved. Tell Troughton to try again tomorrow, because it might be earlier. Anyhow all the times want checking up.*
4. *There is no real proof that anyone was anywhere. Apart from Benson's shifty evidence.*
5. *Do you use brass scrap to make darts?*
6. *Why is this girl Cynthia Trent dodging me?*

7. *Suppose Reeves did do it, he would be just the sort of man to make the muddles in para 1 (above). On the other hand he would have something more than that to get out of it. Because I think that that conceited ass thinks that he can have fun and games with me and get away with it.*
8. *In that case why has he got no alibi?*
9. *You watch it turn up.*

PART IV

"Heedless of grammar, they all cried, 'That's him!'"

— INGOLDSBY LEGENDS.

Mr Pennington shifted uneasily in his chair and pressed the tips of his fingers together. "It is not easy, Inspector, not at all easy. The Department hates forcing its way in. In fact we will not do it. All you tell me is that there is something wrong with the Company and you want me to press our investigations just at this moment. Is that correct?"

"I want all the information that I can get about the Company. I see from the papers in Foster's flat that you were not happy about them. I want to know why?"

"All the papers are at your disposal. But the only cause of our uneasiness officially is that the Department thinks that their labour costs were too high. Mr Foster was told to investigate and, on the whole, he satisfied himself that there was nothing wrong."

"And are you satisfied with this investigation?" Hardwick watched Pennington wriggle in his chair and pressed his point further. "It would not look well if at this juncture *we* found something wrong with their accounts which you had failed to notice."

"It will not look well if anything at all is found wrong with the Company's accounts. I confess, Inspector, that I devoutly hope that everything *is* all right. Why if it got out of the hands of the Ministry and was mentioned by the Controller and Auditor-General to the Public Accounts Committee, why almost anything might happen!" Pennington shuddered. He preferred a quiet life any day and the contingency was too appalling for contemplation.

"I quite understand your position" (Hardwick tried to sound sympathetic), "but don't you think that you would improve it by making the fullest enquiries?"

"Oh, I do, I do! But it is an absolute rule of the Department that we *never* visit a contractor unless it is quite convenient to him."

"And to you?" Hardwick was not going to allow the Ministry to get away with so sweeping a claim to considerateness as was implied.

"As to us, one day is — usually — as good as another. Unless there is some reason for urgency that we can give. But in this case, I hardly feel that I can quote you as our reason. In fact you tell me that we are not to mention you."

"Surely Foster's death makes a reason?"

"For telling someone else to take over the work, yes. I suppose that will be necessary." In a brief parenthesis Hardwick admitted the necessity while Pennington went on blandly ignoring his own understatement. "Yes, and moreover desirable. A change is long overdue. It was quite clear that Mr Foster was too — how shall I put it? — close to that firm. I am not, mind you, Inspector, implying any actual malpractices on his part, but this lunch of which you tell me — shocking, shocking. I can foresee that the office instructions on the subject will be very considerably tightened up. If the press makes any considerable reference to the case, there may even be public comment. Most undesirable, most undesirable."

"Surely that is a good reason for a further and detailed examination on your part?"

"Yes, yes. But the rest of the day — at least perhaps one particular reason for the Company being visited at this time. Indeed what Mr Foster was doing there yesterday, I hardly know. There was no work outstanding with them. Really it is quite beyond me to know what he was doing there."

This was almost too much for the Inspector. It seemed to be altogether too naïve. "Apparently," he said, "he was having lunch with them."

"Yes, yes. But the rest of the day — at least perhaps I should say the morning. The afternoon, unfortunately, we know all about. No doubt Mr Foster had some other appointment in mind when Mr — ah yes, Reeves — left him. But I must admit I am puzzled as to the morning."

"He probably spent it standing in a fish shop queue. Oh don't look shocked. We all have to do it and I don't know that he did, but whatever he was doing, he was not with the Shergold Engineering Company."

"But really, Inspector, look! Our office board on which accountants record the telephone numbers of those whom they are visiting. It shows that he *was* there. So you see—"

Hardwick gave it up. "And what do you think he did there?"

"Ah, there indeed I am defeated. If only I did. If I had some reason for going there…Because I agree with you very largely, Inspector. I am very anxious to go to their offices myself and know everything. But you can see that it is a most awkward time. One director — shall we say away? Not the one most concerned with our side of the Company, I know, but it must throw extra work on the other. The staff, no doubt, a little upset by what has happened. We had a young lady round here yesterday. Very upset, she seemed, in fact at the end she broke down, Inspector. Positively broke down. I fear that rumours may have reached the outer office." Pennington shook his head sadly. It was not good for discipline that he should be laughed at.

"Indeed? And who was the young lady?"

"A Miss Trent."

"So that was where she was. I was looking for her."

"Really? I had no idea — I do hope that her presence here did not in any way inconvenience you. Of course I had no notion—"

"Naturally." Hardwick soothed away the anxious protestations and enquired, "What was the object of her visit?"

"Well, she came with a long story which she got from one of the night-shift. It was all the merest hearsay. At the time it sounded very convincing but thinking it over afterwards I hardly see how I can follow it up. I should like to do so, but I don't see how to open the matter with the Company without giving offence. Mr Shergold, I understand, takes offence easily — at least so Mr Foster said. Of course I shall see that the Department is informed, verbally I expect, and I doubt if any more contracts will be sent to them, but beyond that…"

Hardwick saw a chance and decided to take it. "That hardly sounds fair, sir, if I may say so. You tell me that it was a rumour and that you cannot establish its truth. So you propose to take action which will penalise the Company without giving them the chance to prove it to be untrue. Now both you and the Department would I am sure hate to do anything unfair."

"Of course, of course, naturally. I quite see your point. But how am I to start?"

Hardwick smiled. "I am not an accountant, and, in any case, you have not yet told me what the allegations are which Miss Trent made."

"Oh she hardly made them herself. She passed them on and by the way, she did not give me permission to detail them to you. Certainly she did not authorise me to tell the name of her informant. I really think that you should ask her."

"I shall. But if you would give me a general idea?"

"First of all there was a point about wages. She seemed hardly to be aware what she was saying, but it did put a few ideas into my head—"

"—which you will proceed to investigate?"

"In due course. But it would be so awkward now — to rake up the past just at this moment! In any case it would be a matter which would have to be handled with the greatest tact. To go down to a firm that I have had no personal dealings with before — and I should have to do it myself; I could not think of sending any of my subordinates — in order to make allegations which might not be true. Most unpleasant! Really *most* unpleasant. At such a time too. They would not want to see me."

"No doubt. Indeed I have come across something of the sort myself before now," Hardwick commented drily. "But apart from the wages the allegations were…?"

"You really must ask Miss Trent. Very generally they concerned themselves with a suggestion that the Company was making little articles for civilian consumption with labour and material provided by us. The same allegations have been put forward elsewhere and pretty generally found to be untrue. In this case, perhaps the statements are more circumstantial, though I have known them to be most detailed elsewhere and at the same time quite without foundation. Everything she said too was mere hearsay. I really think that if you spoke to her…"

"But are you not going to investigate these charges, allegations, call them what you will?"

"Well, well, I suppose we must. But perhaps not now: On the first occasion when I get an opportunity to make an excuse to visit them, I will look into it. Oh yes, fully. But, not now. It would hardly be kind to go now."

"Was Mr Foster's death 'kind'?"

"Well, as a matter of fact, so far as I was concerned, he was not a very satisf — Really! Inspector. I do not think that that was a remark that you ought to have made. No, really, you upset me.

I started to say something that I should not have done. I must carefully consider the whole question of when I next visit the Company and the line I shall then take."

For a moment Hardwick thought that he was defeated. No doubt time might cause the representative of the Ministry to do what he wanted him to do. But could he afford to give him that time? On the other hand trying to hustle a Government Department is usually recognised as one of the most certain ways of wasting your energy. His next reaction, possibly influenced by a trace of irritation, was to threaten very gently by making a suggestion that Mr Pennington might be subpoenaed to give evidence, but he dismissed that at once from his mind. Mr Pennington might look very mild, he might have difficulty in making up his mind, but once he was even in appearance threatened, he would almost certainly get his official hackles up and nothing on earth would ever induce him to allow the Ministry — his own admired and feared Ministry, to be coerced. He would not regard it as decent and he would become completely uncooperative. The matter must be left to time. At any rate Mr Pennington must be given time, and, in the meanwhile, Hardwick had plenty of other things to do. With luck Miss Trent might prove more helpful.

The silence, as Hardwick thought, was beginning to become noticeable and finally he had to break into his own meditations. "Perhaps then we had better leave it at that for the moment. I should be glad though if you would think it over."

"Certainly, certainly. Now where did you put your hat? Ah here we are." Hardwick's hat, with a little dust added, was retrieved and he found himself very gently pushed towards the door. Just as he reached it, a further thought struck him. He had already said goodbye, but he permitted himself one last question. "Oh I nearly forgot. There was a small point that I wanted to ask you. Can you make darts out of brass scrap?"

The effect on Pennington was noticeable. "Darts!" he gasped. "Did you say 'darts'?"

"Why, yes." Light suddenly dawned on Hardwick. "I see." He whistled gently. "Articles for civilian consumption? Is that the great idea?" Pennington could only nod. Very carefully Hardwick replaced his hat on top of a stack of files. "Now supposing we both come clean?" he suggested.

Mr Pennington was shocked at the expression but at least collaboration was assured. He positively oozed assistance. "With this additional point to start from, I really think, Inspector, that I am entitled to insist on further investigation. As a matter of urgency moreover. Let me see, today is Friday. I think that I will ring up now and try to make an appointment with them for quite an early day next week. Or perhaps the week after."

Hardwick shook his head. The Ministry's idea of "urgency" and his own did not agree. "No," he said. "You come down without warning and you come down now. Moreover you come down with me." '

"But really, Inspector! The agglomeration of the two visits! This is not the way in which the Ministry *ever* behaves. We *pride* ourselves on being reasonable, on being as little of a nuisance as is possible, on preserving a high standard, compatible of course with efficiency, of good manners, consideration and courtesy. Such a visit as you suggest would be altogether unprecedented."

"And on how many other occasions have you had one of your accountants murdered?"

"Well, yes. I must admit that the circumstances *are* a little unusual."

"Exactly. Come along."

It was an order. Mr Pennington left his other appointments uncared for. He forgot even to say that he was going out. Not that it mattered for the "outer office," even if its discipline was going to the dogs, was taking the greatest interest in all his doings. Fancy Penny going off with the police! For the youngest office girl had spotted who Hardwick was in a moment. By lunch time it was confidently asserted that Penny had been arrested for having himself murdered Foster. Public opinion on the whole was in his favour. It was generally conceded that Foster had given him ample provocation and that to remove him had been a very public-spirited and patriotic action.

* * *

CYNTHIA TRENT HAD AGAIN PASSED A THOROUGHLY bad night. "And if I don't make up my mind soon," she said to herself, "I suppose that I shall go on passing bad ones. I thought that I was going to clear up some of the problems when I passed on to the Ministry what Yabsley had told me. But I fancy that I am only at the beginning of that. Moreover if it is true, it seems to me that the Company will go broke and if it is not and they find out my part in it, I shall get the sack. That is if one can get the sack these days. It's not at all clear to me after yesterday whether you can or cannot. Nor am I sure whether one can resign. I think not in theory and yes in practice — if you are prepared to risk getting called up — and with the war nearly over, I *am* inclined to risk it because while I liked working here, while I thought we were doing something useful, when it comes to helping to make darts — Besides, can one go on receiving quite a good salary after taking the line with the Ministry that I have taken?

"But most difficult of all to decide is whether I show Guy's letter to the police. The question to my mind is simply this. Does it really help him or not? If he had only said in it somewhere 'of course I haven't done it really,' then I should know what to do!" That such a criterion might be one which might not appeal to the police did not occur to her. It did however pass through her mind that apparently Guy wanted the police to think that he had done it — for a while anyhow. But had that while ended? It was all very difficult.

Nor were things easy at the office. To begin with "King Arthur" was in an appalling temper. Given his head, he would have sacked half the staff in haste and possibly repented at leisure, but that being impossible in war time, he had to confine himself to being sarcastic to everyone. She found him bullying the wages clerk until the poor girl was nearly in tears. Cynthia's arrival provided that young woman at least with relief, since Shergold changed the subject of his wrath.

"Ah Miss Trent. Punctual as usual!" (She was five minutes late, practically never had been late before and anyhow had his own leave to be absent all day if she wanted to be so.) "You will find quite a number of people looking for you. Indeed for all of us in turn. You had better be ready with a very full account of when you were born, what your religion is, why your mother's Christian name was Anastasia Euphrosyne—"

"But it wasn't."

"I never said it was. But you will have to explain it all to Inspector Hardwick's two bone-headed and not in the least budding detectives. In particular you will have to say everything that you did on Wednesday. Not that it is anything to do with them but 'it is just a routine matter,' they will tell you. When I next see that Inspector I am going to suggest that he gets out a form for future murders and gets everyone to fill it up. I believe that we could do it more rapidly for ourselves instead of, as at present, giving the police the information with which to fill it up."

"Is the Inspector here at present? I think that I should like to get it over." It would at any rate, though she did not say so, be preferable to talking to "King Arthur" and it certainly could not give her a worse headache.

"No. But you can talk to both his myrmidons. You have to talk to them together though. In case, I suppose, you shock them."

"Oh well. No doubt they will come to see me if they want to."

Cynthia settled down for the day's work and was relieved to see that Shergold took the hint. At any rate he went back to his own office.

Her movements on the Wednesday! There was nothing of interest in that. In fact so far as she was concerned the only thing of interest which had occurred to her was that Guy had written to her. When she came to think of it, why had he not given her that letter? The answer of course came to her at once. He had not wanted her to get it until the next morning. To tell or not to tell, that was still her question.

In fact her conversation with Hardwick's "myrmidons" was of the shortest and least interesting. She hugged to herself the idea that she was going to get away with it lightly at any rate for that day. Perhaps they would not come on Saturday and after the weekend, surely, she could make up her mind. At any rate her head might stop aching.

Just however, as routine was making the office of the Shergold Engineering Company less dynamic, a fresh and very vigorous centre of disturbance descended upon them, or at any rate upon Arthur Shergold. All that the office knew at first was that the Inspector was back with them again and that this time he was accompanied by a mild man in the early fifties. In appearance, he was not unlike the Inspector, and, at first, he was thought to be yet another member of Scotland Yard. It was generally considered by the younger members of the female staff that the Yard was letting itself down. It ought to have at least *one* large and really burly man and somebody ought to be knocked about, bullied and reduced to tears. Instead of which they were all immensely polite and left the bullying to their own employer. It was disappointing. A second look at the Inspector's companion produced further disappointment. He was carrying a black leather bag with the Royal Cypher on it. Mr Foster had carried a similar one. Apparently, he was only another official of the Ministry.

There might be interesting developments but on the whole the office expected that it would be dull. Meanwhile, it reserved judgment.

Shergold however did not find it dull, nor did he suspend judgment. He had begun to complain before Hardwick had explained who his companion was. "Oh good morning, Inspector," he said in a tone which implied anything but pleasure at seeing him. "Surely there is nothing more that I can do for you?"

"Not at this exact moment," was the equable and almost priggish reply. "I have only to see what my subordinates have done and perhaps ask a few questions of some of your employees. I am sure that I may?"

"If you must, I suppose you must."

"Thank you," Hardwick ignored the curtness of a permission which anyhow was only asked for as a courtesy on his part. He supposed that if a man habitually lived in the stifling and airless heat continually affected by Shergold, he was likely to be bad tempered. "But before I deal with my own affairs, I want to introduce Mr Pennington from the Ministry who has come down with me."

Shergold glanced rudely at the little man, but failing to make any impression on him, he was reduced into putting his discourtesy into words. "Ah! So I see. Just before lunch." The mild Mr Pennington blushed at the innuendo. He was rather self-conscious on the subject of lunch at the moment. But Hardwick was not at all abashed. "I should rather think that officials of the Ministry would be shy of lunching with your Company this week. However, as a matter of fact, we took a sandwich on the way down and so we need not worry you."

"I see. That not being the object for what purpose am I indebted to this visit of Mr Pennington's?"

The repetition of the same suggestion seemed so crude to the man thus asked that he forgot his shyness and began almost brusquely. "The unfortunate death of Mr Foster — and may I say that I think a word of condolence with his employers would not have been out of place in the circumstances—"

"If you are trying to pretend to me for a moment that the Ministry mind—"

"—will not obviate the necessity for the examination of your accounts."

"I never imagined that it would have any result so fortunate. On the other hand fortune is with me at this moment in that I believe that every contract which we have been so unlucky as to have from you is not only finished but investigated or placed on a fixed price basis. It is true that you have not seen our last annual accounts, those for 1944, and I should very much like to call your attention to those one day. They show, as has been the unfortunate predicament of many of those who have devoted themselves heart and soul to working for the Ministry, increased work and decreased profits. You persuade us to take an estimated rate of overheads and when that proves, as it only too often does, to be too low, you are not interested. Nor are we amused."

Pennington was fairly stung at the injustice of the assorted charges, but he had no desire to undertake the detailed defence of his Department at that particular moment. A few general words however could not be avoided. "I can assure you that it is not our wish to treat anyone harshly and perhaps on some other occasion you may afford me the opportunity of going into it. But this would hardly be a suitable time."

"On that at least we can agree. A more unsuitable time for you to come here it is not possible to imagine. You must be capable of conceiving some idea of how I am placed at the moment."

"Certainly."

"Yet you have come. Why?"

Faced with having to make what must clearly be at least tentative accusations of fraud, Pennington began to stutter. In the end it was Hardwick who had to take up the tale. "In the late Mr Foster's papers, which of course it was my duty to read through, there were suggestions that the wages system was not altogether what it should be. I called Mr Pennington's attention to these."

"But Mr Foster has not looked at the wages system for ages!"

Pennington recovered himself and thinking that he saw an opening took up the conversation. "That is true. In fact really that is exactly the point. He seems to have looked at them in a very lax way. And with all the attention that is likely to be paid to this Company, I am simply bound to look into the whole thing again and at once. Of course I am very sorry to give you any trouble but there it is. It is my obvious duty and I am sure that you would desire that I should carry it out."

"I could not possibly imagine anything in which I am less interested in than you and your duty. Do I really understand that you want to go into my wages at this moment?"

"I am afraid so." Pennington looked miserable.

"I have never concealed anything, and you are perfectly at liberty to look at what you want. I shall however please myself as to whether I complain to the Ministry as to your complete lack of consideration." Seeing that this threat apparently produced no impression, he went on sulkily, "How far back do you want the wages book. Six months?"

"I might have to go further back than that."

A snort was the first answer, followed by a surly permission to ask for what he wanted. Mr Pennington remained mildness itself. "I should like," he said in a very gentle voice, "all the wages books in your safe as well as those in the wages office."

There was a moment of silence and then Shergold, in a voice of icy coldness, asked if he was implying that there would be different wages books in one to the other. "Not in the least," was the answer, "but it is very usual to put the old books away. If you would open the safe…"

"And if I refuse? Have you, or has the Inspector, got a search warrant?"

"I could not speak for the Inspector, but I have a card here covering the matter generally. You see that it shows that I am a person authorised by the Ministry to inspect your accounts for any period which I may consider necessary. The Ministry are empowered to require production of books and documents under Regulation 55 (1) of the Defence (General) Regulations 1939."

Hardwick, with difficulty, suppressed a cheer. He had not himself thought of that one. Seeing that Shergold looked as if for the moment he had no reply, Pennington, though the beads of sweat on his forehead were not entirely due to the airless room, pressed on. "I want also to go into the question of scrap on various contracts. It has come to our notice that a great deal has been sold by you and I am bound to satisfy myself that due credit has been given for it. That will involve examining a ledger or two of yours. Possibly also some of those men who worked on the contract."

Shergold shrugged his shoulders. "What on earth is this country coming to! Of all the appalling inquisitions! I really shall have to write to the Ministry and congratulate them on their sense of timing. To wait until one of the two directors of a Company is charged with murder — on his own confession—" He seized a piece of paper and began to write.

Dear Sirs,

SALE OF SCRAP.

My co-director made a statement the day before yesterday to Scotland Yard. In it he said that he murdered one of your accountants. This moment has been chosen by a senior official of the same branch of your Ministry to investigate the above question.

LEFT-HANDED DEATH

I hope that you are pleased with the admirable timing—

He threw down his pen and shoved the paper to Pennington. "That is only a rough draft. I shall get it better in a short while. Meanwhile I think that you had better work next door. It used to be our fire-watcher's room and as it is now not used you will not be disturbed. Meanwhile here are my keys. The books and records are at your disposal." He threw the keys dramatically on the table and turned to the Inspector. "And what can I do for you?"

"Oh nothing." Hardwick was all mildness. "I should just like to talk to Miss Trent if I might."

"Oh just as you please. Make yourselves at home, both of you. Have all the books and the staff up and have a good time. Only don't worry about me, will you?"

"No, sir." Butter would not have melted in Hardwick's mouth. Shergold gave him one contemptuous glance. "In that case," he said, "I think I shall go out to lunch. I may as well take my time. It is obviously quite impossible for anyone here to do any work."

* * *

"So this is how the poor fire-watched!" Hardwick looked round at a comfortably furnished room. It had even a divan bed in the corner.

Pennington pursed his lips. "I suspect only the directors and senior office staff. But if you come to that not everyone was content latterly to do their fire-watching on the top floor."

"True. Still *we* aren't allowed such luxury. A comfortable chair, a desk to work at. Books. A bed. There is even a first-aid cupboard. Now I wonder what they kept in that."

"First-aid things, I suppose." Pennington was hardly listening to the Inspector. He was keeping an eye all the time on the safe in Shergold's room, for though Shergold was supposed to have gone out to lunch, you could never be quite sure. A little fussily, Pennington supervised a clerk bringing a stack of books to the fire-watching room and putting them on the table. Then he gave instructions for such other records and accounts as he thought that they might need to be brought and finally settled down to what he expected to be a laborious and rather tricky afternoon's work. Of one thing he was quite certain. If he was ever going to find anything wrong with the books of the Shergold Engineering Company, it would be on that afternoon.

At first there was complete silence. Then Pennington became aware of curious little scratchings as if a piece of wire was scraping against a piece of wood. That was followed by small satisfied chirping noises from Hardwick. Disturbed in adding up a column of figures Pennington looked up a little testily. "What *is* it, Inspector? If I can help you, I shall be most willing, but you must excuse me if I say that you are just a little distracting."

"Sorry. But this is an awfully interesting medicine cupboard."

"Really? I don't think that I have ever heard a medicine cupboard called that before. In what way is it interesting?"

"It has got two wine glasses in it and some drinks."

"But you wouldn't suggest —I say, you haven't opened it?"

"He told us to make ourselves at home."

"But he cannot have meant that. I thought it was locked."

"So it was." The Inspector was blandness itself. "You wouldn't like a drink?"

"My dear Inspector!"

"I forgot — your conscience. Besides there is no claret here. There is some rum though. And lots and lots of bottles."

"First-aid, I suppose. Bandages. Morphia tablets."

"That sort of thing." Hardwick's assent was vague and non-committal. "I wonder what they wanted with Codeine Co though."

"Codeine Co?"

"Codeine compositum — not company. You can get tablets containing it at any manufacturing chemists. The amount of codeine in it is so small that you do not even have to sign the poison register. It just gives you a nice sleep, that's all."

"I suppose that their fire-watchers needed it. Many people are quite unable to sleep when they are in a strange place."

"But I thought that fire-watchers were supposed to stay awake?"

"I have not always noticed that to be so," Pennington answered drily. "And sleep being a necessity, it seems to me to be quite a reasonable thing for them to have."

"I suppose so. I say, am I disturbing you?"

"Well…" It was too obvious for Mr Pennington to deny the fact.

"Yes, all right. I'll just put the cupboard back as I found it and then I shall go in search of the fair Cynthia. I think that I shall have to use Mr Shergold's own office for the purpose. Let's hope he is having a very good lunch and will not need it for a bit."

When Cynthia arrived, he looked at her curiously. The fair, rather ordinary type of pretty girl such as she was made very little impression on him. He was more interested in the fact that she was obviously tired and worried, and he was shrewd enough too to see that there was a determined look on her face. She could be very loyal and very obstinate probably, if she wanted to be.

"Miss Trent?" he said. "I was not able to find you yesterday."

"No. I — it hardly occurred to me that you would want to. I was upset — naturally — and Mr Shergold gave me leave to go away. Then I started worrying and I went round to see the Ministry. As Mr Pennington came here with you, I suppose he has told you what I said."

"Yes. In the end, I have been told all about the naughty night-shift and their wicked employer. The proof of that mainly concerns Mr Pennington and is in his hands. Still I find it interesting. Perhaps after Mr Pennington has investigated — I don't know. But as a matter of fact do you believe in it yourself?"

"I — I hardly know. Of one thing I am quite sure: Mr Reeves knew nothing about it."

"You liked Mr Reeves, didn't you?"

"Yes. Why shouldn't I?"

"No reason at all. I just wanted to know."

"Are you sort of making insinuations, Inspector? Because if so, I ought to tell you that the last person who made such insinuations in this room had his face smacked."

"Oh!" Hardwick rubbed his cheek and remembered that he had seen Shergold doing just that. "He did, did he? The idea that Mr Reeves was jealous of Mr Foster seems to be quite a prevalent one, I understand. I am sorry if I am putting it bluntly, but I do not believe in being coy and I don't think you do either."

"I believe that you ought not to say things like that. But whether you ought or not, it is quite nonsense. There never was the tiniest anything between Mr Foster and myself. I was polite to him. It was part of my job. After all, these people from the Ministry are all right and quite fair, but all the same it can do no harm to keep on the right side of them. It's a bit sick-making at times because they get oily and think they are being ever so kind and helpful when all that you really want is to see the back of them. Foster was very much that way. He wasn't much trouble though, I will say that for him, and I admit that I used to keep him smoothed down, so to speak. But that was all."

"And was that all there was between you and Mr Reeves?"

Cynthia blushed. "In fact, yes. Though people will keep saying things. To be honest, Inspector, I rather fancy that we were both wondering if we were interested in the other and we had neither of us made up our minds. I was sorry for him. His hand for one thing and then I thought that Mr Shergold was beastly to him. He pushed him aside all the time and he was always running him down by implication and being a bit sarcastic about him behind his back. Guy would have hated it if he had known, but then Guy is so terribly vain."

"So I had noticed."

"Well, anyone would. That was one of the reasons that made me hesitate. I was sorry for him and I had tried to look after his affairs while he was away, but that was really all — then."

"And now?"

"Well, would you expect me to turn round and desert him now?"

Hardwick looked at her deeply. "I'll be just. I should *not* expect you to. But all the same I have a sort of idea that you might do something stupid. You might hold back something. To be honest, I have no reason to think that you are doing so and no grounds for saying so, but I have a hunch that you are. For one thing, though it does not necessarily mean a thing, you dodged me too carefully yesterday."

For a minute there was silence. Then Cynthia said, "Do you mind if we open the window? Mr Shergold always keeps the room most frightfully hot. I don't believe that he ever thinks for a moment that other people may not like it. I don't like draughts myself in the way that Guy does, but all the same…"

Hardwick got up and opened it for her. "Mr Shergold," he said, "is sure to hate it but after all he told me to make myself at home." Then he sat down again and faced Cynthia squarely. "Well?" he said.

Cynthia had evidently been thinking fast. "Inspector," she said, "in how much danger is Guy?"

It was a fair enough question to anyone else but Inspector Hardwick. Nevertheless it got a fair reply. "He has confessed to a crime which in fact was done. The knowledge that it had been done was shared so far as we know by very few people. He has given a detailed account of how he did it. So far, though that account is not wholly corroborated, it has not proved to be entirely wrong anywhere—"

"But he says that it is wrong in some places," Cynthia broke in without quite thinking what she was saying.

"And how do you know that?" Hardwick clearly interested, sat bolt upright.

"Oh!" Too late Cynthia realised what she had done.

"Have you seen him since?"

"No."

"Written to you?" Cynthia wriggled uneasily in her chair and emitted a faint "yes." Then she pulled herself together. "Oh! I suppose I had better put a good face on it. Here's the letter and I hope you like it. I didn't think, Inspector, that you were the sort of man to catch me out that way."

"You haven't known me long." Hardwick murmured gently as he began to read the pages. "Yes, yes, I see. To some extent that explains the business about lunch. Also the fact that we have not found the bus conductor or conductress who saw him. You know I am afraid that this does not help him very much. I shall have to keep it, of course and look into all the details. Perhaps — oh! Do not cry, Miss Trent. You did that to Mr Pennington yesterday, and I understand that he will never live it down. All right, all right, I was a beast to make you produce it and perhaps it will help him. Though I am by no means certain that he is as anxious to be helped as I am to help him." The speech was a longer one than he was accustomed to make and, becoming aware of that, he was slightly irritated. Besides he never could stand young women who cried. Ignoring the bewilderment on her face caused by the last phrase which was wholly meaningless to anyone who did not know his determination to prove Reeves innocent, he folded the letter up and put it back into its envelope. Suddenly he stopped and looked at it again. "There it is!" he exclaimed suddenly.

"There *what* is?" Cynthia sounded a little cross. She hated people who spoke in riddles.

"The alibi. I knew it was going to turn up." He looked at the envelope slowly and then continued.

"I gather that he posted this himself. At least so he implies. And it was posted at the office just opposite according to the postmark. No one has said that he asked him or her to post a letter for him. Oh! But I suppose that you posted this yourself?"

"I certainly did not." Then seeing that he looked dubious, she went on, "I can see your difficulty in believing me and if I knew what the point was, I quite grant you that I should be fully prepared to lie. It sounds as if I am helping Guy by saying I did not post it, but you might be laying a trap for me. How am I to know? You seem to be quite capable of doing so."

"Ah! I told you we should get to know each other better."

Cynthia shuddered. "I hope *not*," she said firmly. "Anyhow you can be sure of one thing. I give you my most solemn word of honour that I did not post that letter myself, that it arrived just as it is in that envelope and that so far as I know no one else, other than Guy, is aware of its existence."

"I see. In return for that piece of frankness and to make up for any — ah, doubts you may have of my bona-fides, I will give you a little information. I happened to notice that the post office opposite has a collection at 1.30 and 2.30. This is post-marked 2.30. Of course you cannot be quite sure these days with post offices but apparently this letter was posted here by Mr. Reeves after 1.30 and before 2.30."

"But — but — I don't quite understand."

"You think it over. Perhaps you had better answer that telephone. It is more likely to be for Mr Shergold than for me."

Cynthia picked up the receiver. "No," she said after a moment or so, "it's for you. It's — Oh, he won't give a name."

"Thank you. That will be all Miss Trent for the present. But please stay where I can find you." He bowed her out of the room and started to listen to what Sergeant Matthews had to say.

* * *

SERGEANT MATTHEWS WAS in fact very plaintive. Everybody, it appeared, had snubbed him. He had made every effort to get Doctor Grantham's report and was merely told by Doctor Grantham's secretary that the police were very lucky to have the services of a grossly overworked doctor who had all his partner's patients to look after as well as his own. The doctor had authorised her to say that he very much doubted if he would be able to take on any further work for them. Matthews had contented himself with saying that he hoped that there would be no need. "And I did not say that the desire to part was mutual. After all, Maida Vale is not a district where we get many murders."

"Your idea entirely," Hardwick told him. "I don't think that I have ever looked at it in that way. We might get out one of those shaded maps showing the incidence of murders per thousand people in the district."

"Yes, sir." Matthews never understood anything that was not a serious statement. "And then there's Reeves. He's begun to create."

"What's biting him?"

"Well, to tell you the truth, I think he's feeling a trifle neglected. Having cast himself for the leading part in this drama of his own making—"

"If it is his."

"Well, the confessing was his idea anyhow — he does *not* approve of anyone else having a look in. He asked to see me just now and put all sorts of questions to me as to where you were. Of course I gave him no sort of reply whereupon he flew into a real temper about it. It was a scandal, he would take it up with the Commissioners of Police, the delays of justice were intolerable, you were wasting his and your time, especially his."

"Grand. And what exactly does he expect me to have done?"

"Curiously enough he is a little uncertain about that. I fancy that he has several different ends to his drama. In one he is proved innocent most triumphantly and magnanimously declines to bring an action against us for false imprisonment. In another he is reprieved at the gallows-foot by means of a proof dramatically revealed at the last moment—"

"Really? I think I know what that one is. I suspect it is one that I have just come across. But go on."

"Is that so, sir? The third ending I fancy is that he is hanged — preferably publicly but he knows that that is hard to manage these days. With the result that he hardly has the matter worked out to his satisfaction. But really I would be glad to have something to keep him quiet with."

"I think I can provide you with that." Very briefly Hardwick told Matthews of a letter being received by Cynthia Trent and ended by saying, "Sound him about this letter and find out what his story is about posting it. I purposely have not told you the contents and details yet. It would only confuse you and I want to get his reactions from someone who does not know the whole significance. Clear?"

"Quite clear but there is just one more thing. Troughton has been up to Cricklewood again as you told him and seen the conductresses who were on the earlier buses. The identification is not very good, but I gather he has some scrap of news. Shall I put him on the phone?"

"Yes."

"Just a minute." A brief conversation with the switchboard operator preceded Troughton's voice. "I proceeded this morning, sir, to the garage at Cricklewood for the purpose of interviewing the conductresses of number sixty buses who passed Piccadilly Circus between one and two in the afternoon of

Wednesday, April 18th, instead of those who passed that point between two and three in the afternoon of the same day. I had interviewed the two to three group on the previous day without success.

"I took with me the prescribed photographs leaving out one of which an identification of an unrequired nature had been made yesterday. One conductress has made a rather doubtful identification of the photograph of Foster with his head thrown back. She said that she remembered the startled look on his face and has an idea that the man looked about as surprised as that when his companion allowed him to pay for the tickets. She is not sure and might break down if pressed. She can give no description of the companion and the photograph of Reeves does not seem to convey anything to her. I introduced gently the subject of putting the ticket emphatically in the box, but she remembered nothing of that. She says that lots of people do that, busybodies in her opinion who want to point out to other people that they have done so and therefore are superior people to those who have not. For that matter she says that many people are surprised when their companions only fumble and others are surprised when they are asked to pay at all. Still she did pick up Foster if only hesitatingly. It is not very much, I am afraid, sir. In fact it only amounts to the fact that she did half identify Foster in connection with a companion and the taking of a ticket. I have particulars of her and know where to get her."

"Quite right," said Hardwick, "and her bus passed the stop in Regent Street opposite Oddenino's at what time?"

"The stop is a few yards north of there. It was due there at 1.32 and she says that they were fairly accurate on time all the way."

"I see. That will be all for the moment. Make your report on that straight away."

He put down the receiver. So Foster, who was lunching at Oddenino's between 1.45 and 2.15 after drinking cocktails there from 1.30 to 1.45 had got on a sixty bus at 1.32 and gone back from Oddenino's towards Maida Vale. He wondered if Troughton had found out where he got off. "Next the man who has confessed to his murder has told me that he took him on a sixty bus about quarter-past two and gives a hint of trouble as to who paid of the kind that the conductress noticed. Or rather of something of the kind but not exactly trouble at the same moment. In a private letter which I suspect was really intended to reach me, he carefully explains that a point in his defence will be that there will be no trace of him on the bus because in fact they went by taxi. I think that Troughton had better follow up his bus success by going through the taxis. It only remains to find that he went by taxi and the whole thing will be perfectly clear."

Just as he was about to ring up Troughton once more, the telephone went again. Hardwick answered it discreetly but found that it was not for Shergold as he had expected but for Pennington. He fetched him from the next room and found him not too pleased to be disturbed. "I think," he told the Inspector quietly as he went to the telephone, "mind you I only think, that I am finding about the wages of this Company once upon a time. Seems to be all right now though." He put his mouth to the receiver and said, "Pennington speaking."

"This is the Private Secretary to the Permanent Secretary to the Ministry here. So glad to get hold of you. Might I have your advice? It is about your Mr Foster. A very sad matter. No doubt a useful member of your staff?"

"We...ell." Pennington's honesty compelled him to stutter for a minute. The more he investigated the books of the Shergold's Engineering Company the less he was convinced of Foster's utility.

But the cheerful young voice swept on. "Of course normally I should not worry the Permanent Secretary about such a matter but on reading the newspapers I rather gather that Mr

Foster lost his life very gallantly trying to get information from a Company whom he had reason to believe might turn nasty about it. Of course if that is so the Secretary might want the Department's official regrets sent to his family. Has he any family by the way?"

"No very close relation so far as I know. But I will look into it if you like."

"I only want to trouble you if it is necessary. You see we have to be rather careful as to what we say because if he was killed in the course of his duty, then the Department might be liable, and I don't know what view the Treasury would make of that, but I think one might fairly assume that they would object. That is generally a pretty sound assumption. In that case of course it would be a pity if there had been any communication from us expressing regret, even of the most general kind — even though that expression would naturally not admit liability. On the other hand the circumstances are unusual, and we do not want to appear to be discourteous. I haven't spoken to the Secretary yet. What do you think?"

"Mr Foster appears to have been killed," Pennington answered a little tartly, "after taking far too good a lunch at a moment when he should have been working. He seems to have known the Company far too well personally and to have failed to have found out about its accounts. At least, I hope so, for he certainly failed to tell me about it if he did. As to the motive, it is not yet clear who did it."

"I thought that there had been a confession."

"Which the police are still checking up. I have no idea whether they are satisfied yet with it, but they certainly do not seem satisfied with the Company. Nor am I. There is also some suggestion going about locally that the motive might have been a personal one. I just do not know. But the whole thing seems a bit doubtful. The only thing quite certain is that for the first time Mr Foster will be unable to give an absolutely complete demonstration of his own excessive rectitude. Nothing else but death could ever have stopped him doing that."

"Oh I see! That is a very different story to that which I had imagined. I am most grateful to you. I shall certainly take no action." From the other end an almost red-hot receiver was dropped. Mr Foster's friends would not be comforted by official regrets.

For his part Pennington put down his receiver to find himself confronted with a very angry Shergold. "I admit," he spluttered, "that I invited you two to make yourselves at home, but I thought that it was to be in the room next door and I certainly do not see why you found it necessary to turn the entire room into an icehouse. Except of course that it is obviously desired to make it impossible for me to work today. Fortunately I no longer prepare the weekly wages or their absence on a Friday would cause a strike, or at least a considerable disturbance. In that case we should probably all join your Mr Foster rather rapidly." Very angrily he shut the extremely small crack of window which Hardwick had opened at Cynthia's request. Pennington sighed. He had quite enough reasons of his own to excite Shergold's wrath without becoming the legatee of those of other people.

Back in the room that had once been occupied by the fire-watchers Hardwick was engaged in drawing up a little table.

The first sheet concerned Reeves.

He describes his movements as follows, he wrote:
12.45 Leaves office.
1.30 Reaches Oddenino's.
1.30 to 1.45 Rum cocktails at Oddenino's.
1.45 to 2.15 Lunch at Oddenino's.

Half an hour even at Oddy's means too good service these days to be true, Hardwick thought, *but Reeves gives himself latitude on all these times at both ends. However — to go on.*

> ...
>
> *2.15 to 2.45 Goes to Maida Vale.*
> *3.0 Murders Foster.*
> *3.45 Returns to office.*
> *3.45 to 4.15 Tells Shergold about it and leaves for Scotland Yard.*

The next sheet was headed "Shergold."

> ...
>
> *12.45 Left office. Note. Neither saw the departure of the other, though Shergold thinks Reeves left a bit before one. Why?*
> *1.0 Reaches Elizabeth Street, driving fast.*
> *1.15 to 2.0 Lunch.*
> *2.30 Return to office.*
> *3.45 Shergold comes and talks to him.*

Finally there was a heading "Miscellaneous."

> ...
>
> *1.0 Benson says Shergold talked to him at Elizabeth Street.*
> *3.45 to 1.0 Barman at Oddenino's thinks he served Foster.*
> *1.0 (soon after) Waiter thinks Foster lunched at Oddenino's.*
> *1.32 No. 60 bus boarded opposite Oddenino's by Foster.*
> *2.0 Doctor Grantham thinks Foster was murdered at about this time.*

He put down the sheets and considered that on the whole the contradictions were more interesting than the agreements. Then rather absent-mindedly he picked up a sheet and headed it "Pennington." "As a matter of interest, Mr Pennington," he said, "would you like to account for your movements between let us say twelve and three, on the day before yesterday?"

"No. I mean yes. I wish you wouldn't interrupt." His ejection from Shergold's office had left Pennington a little ruffled. He examined some papers and apparently was going to give no further answer. After a few minutes though he put down his pen. "But now that you have asked, I find that I cannot concentrate until I have told you. My usual habit — no doubt the office are perfectly aware of my habits and can confirm this — is to lunch between twelve-thirty and one-thirty. I find it quite useless to go out later or you get no food and I dislike going earlier. In fact I would rather lunch later, but there it is."

"And you did that on Wednesday?"

"I lunched at my usual restaurant. They would confirm that."

"Quite. In a way this is disappointing. I was hoping to have it confirmed that no one can ever account for his movements forty-eight hours afterwards, but you can. The office staff till twelve-thirty, the restaurant, the office again."

"Well, as a matter of fact, no." Pennington blushed and Hardwick in a rather startled way pulled the sheet of paper to him. "Not?" he queried.

"Well, a very old friend of mine has a son of whom he is always talking. This week the boy is having a week's coaching at Lord's and his father was very keen that someone should see how he is getting on. He kept on asking me to have a look at him as he could not. You know I never like to disappoint anyone and besides the boy is my godson. Not that I really know much about cricket."

"You are *not* going to tell me that you went to Lord's the day before yesterday. And by yourself?"

Pennington nodded. "Yes. The boy's net was from two to half-past. He's quite a promising left-hand bat, I should say. I got there just after he had started—"

"*How did you get there?*"

"I — I am afraid that I completed the journey on a number sixty bus. But only from the Marble Arch."

Hardwick looked at Pennington in a horrified way. If he had finished his lunch shortly before half-past one and then gone to the Marble Arch, he could perfectly well have met Foster somewhere there (unless indeed he had lunched not at his usual restaurant — a point to be checked up — but at Oddenino's and boarded there the bus which had been due to stop north of Piccadilly Circus at 1.32). There would have been time for him to have gone into Foster's flat, got rid of that tiresome, insubordinate and troublesome assistant and gone on to Lord's. In fact if Grantham was right as to the probable time of death, it would fit in quite tidily with the visit to the net at Lord's which no doubt would be confirmed by both the godson and his coach. There was possibility and there was motive. As to the parental pressure which had caused him to go there, no doubt it was true enough. On the other hand it might merely be the suggestion which had prompted the plan — whatever the plan might have been.

On the other hand there were various points which did not tally. The lunch, Reeves' whole action, the letter posted before the crime. Moreover Reeves and Pennington had apparently never met. On the whole it was not a very likely solution. Still he had better get a few more facts, the names and whereabouts, for instance, of the cricketing godson and the proud parent. To all such questions as he asked him, Pennington replied meekly like a small boy caught out in wrongdoing. Indeed in his own opinion, as he freely confessed, he had been doing wrong. He had not got back to the office until very late and that at a time when he was very busy. Moreover he had given to the outer office a wholly untruthful reason for his absence and it was clear that he hoped that the Inspector would not give him away.

But the Inspector was not interested in the amount of work

done for the Ministry. "I hope," he said abruptly, "that you tipped him properly."

"Of course," Pennington answered absent-mindedly from the depths of a calculation to which he had already returned. "Meanwhile may I be allowed to get on with my work?" The Inspector took the hint and quietly absented himself for a short while and did some telephoning of his own.

* * *

LIFE, Detective Constable Troughton thought, was looking up. At Cricklewood he had found something useful. It should do him a bit of good. The next instruction had been dreary. He had interviewed a number of taxi-drivers and discovered nothing except a fact which he had strongly suspected already, namely, that while taxi-drivers may think it wiser to talk to the police freely, they would much prefer not to do so at all. For that matter they would prefer not to waste any time during business hours.

So far then as the particular commission from Hardwick was concerned, he had achieved to date absolutely nothing. But now he was to be taken off it. He was to have a brief morning in the country, not too far from London, solely to ask a few very simple questions. Had the man questioned a son who was being coached at Lord's? Did the boy bat right or left-handed? At what time of day was he being coached? Had the father been unable to go to see him and had he asked anyone else to look in? He was to note anything else said that might be of interest and he was to go to Lord's on Saturday afternoon, see a young man, confirm that he did bat left-handed and that he had had an old friend of his father's looking at him on the Wednesday afternoon who had tipped him. He might, the Inspector had indicated, confirm it to some extent with the coach, but it was pretty sure to be true.

Lord's on a Saturday? Troughton thought. *I don't always get that bit of luck! I hope the coach is one of the real swells. They do sometimes do a bit of coaching at Lord's, I believe. And after that I'm damned if I don't watch the cricket for half an hour or so.* Then he checked himself. It was hot enough. But had cricket started yet? His evening paper was beginning to make some faint reference to it. "When cricket starts at Headquarters in a fortnight's time," it said. Troughton's face fell. There would be nothing to watch but these blooming young gentlemen being coached! "Just my luck to be sent to Lord's a fortnight too soon," he muttered. He made his way back to the Yard humming, "There'll always be an onion." It was what he felt that he was.

AT THE YARD he found Matthews, to whom he reported, in a bad temper. Why had the Inspector taken him, Troughton, off his work on taxis? Even though Troughton could probably be guaranteed to find out nothing, it was the right line, whereas to go running about Lord's sounded preposterous. He even believed that the Inspector had left the offices of the Shergold Engineering Company and gone worrying the Ministry about when one of their people lunched and where. In his, Matthews', opinion Inspector Hardwick ought to be made to lunch off red herrings for a week. "And meanwhile," he concluded, "he leaves me to do the really difficult job and withholds some of the facts. Deliberately withholds them."

Troughton made sympathetic noises which could not however by any possible stretch of exaggeration be turned into words and used in evidence. Even those faint sounds however were sufficient to remind Matthews that he ought not to be talking like that to one of his subordinates about a superior officer. He packed Troughton off quickly.

All the same his interview with Reeves had been quite

enough to throw anyone out of the normal routine of his equanimity.

"I am bound to say, Sergeant," that languid young man had commenced, "that I think very little of this police station. I have passed a most uncomfortable night."

"Possibly it is not exactly our intention to make things excessively comfortable." "Police station" indeed!

"Then it should be. How otherwise is one to give of one's best?"

"You should try a German concentration camp."

"The comparison is yours and otherwise is uncalled for. But what I also complain of is the studious neglect to which I have been subjected. I think that I have mentioned it before."

"You have. Need we go into it again?"

"Since apparently it has made no impression on you, I think that it would be best if we did. I must very definitely remind you that I am much the most important person in this matter—"

"I had thought that Mr Foster—"

"Foster is dead."

"Exactly."

"How then can he be important? Besides he never was a person of any real consequence. It's me that you ought to be concentrating upon. Instead of which you leave me sitting in extremely uncomfortable quarters, doing nothing. Are you doing *anything* about it, Sergeant Matthews?"

"Oh! Yes. Quite a lot. For instance we are checking up most carefully on what you have said to us."

"But I thought that I instructed you to do nothing of the sort?"

"I wonder," Matthews asked shrewdly, "if you really expected us to carry out those instructions? Or indeed to take instructions at all?" Then, seeing that he had produced some effect, he tried to go on diplomatically. "Besides, the story that you told us was a very interesting one. It was bound to rouse our curiosity."

"Yes, yes." Reeves relaxed perceptibly. "No doubt something novel, an original concept, would be bound…" He leant back, so far as it was possible to do so in the rather austere chair provided. Apparently, he was pleased at having provided a bright patch in the drab existences of Inspector Hardwick and Sergeant Matthews. "No doubt you have confirmed everything?"

The question of course was evaded. "One thing of interest — or so I gather — has turned up," Matthews answered, "and that is a letter which you wrote."

"A letter?" Reeves' eyes went hard. "Written to whom?"

"To a Miss Trent, I understand."

"Oh!" Reeves put a great deal of expression into the monosyllable. "Oh *indeed!* So I suppose that is why you have been testing everything that I told you. And how, may I ask, have you prospered?"

"That I am not prepared to tell you at the moment."

"Then I am not at all sure that I am prepared to tell *you,* anything. There must be reciprocity in these matters, Sergeant."

For a moment the tall, black-haired slim man with the graceful and indolent pose of youth and the short, fair, industrious detective, so much more used to receiving the hard knocks of the world, confronted each other in silence. It looked at first as if it might be a conflict of wills but of the two Reeves was always more likely to talk first while Matthews had at all times the greater self-discipline. So it was Reeves who spoke next.

"Now I wonder exactly why you have got that letter at all?" He looked enquiringly at Matthews who having no idea what he meant maintained a silence that gave the appearance of being a deliberate evasion.

"Did Cynthia think it was necessary?" Reeves went on more to himself than to his companion. "Because in that case — she might easily think that things were, shall we say, more definitely settled than in fact — however — but I really hardly think so. Interesting though — if that's the reason." For the first time the full consequences of his action seemed to dawn upon him and an expression of anxiety and uncertainty, wholly foreign in his usual appearance and behaviour, appeared on his face. More to himself than to Matthews he murmured, "Now I wonder which would be most interesting, to be found innocent of a murder that one had committed or guilty of one which one had not?" He seemed to consider that the choice lay wholly with him and that the alternatives were still open to him. His mind was apparently far away and though his lips moved, nothing that he said was audible. He reminded Matthews of one of the little Matthews repeating to himself the repetition that he had been told to learn. Apparently, Reeves was going through again the scenes that dealt with the death of Foster.

Suddenly however he sat up abruptly. "Now I wonder," he said angrily to Matthews, "if Cynthia is double-crossing me? I thought I could trust her but I'm damned if you can ever be sure of a woman. What do you think, Sergeant?" A pause. "Do you never say anything?"

Not having more than a slight notion of what Reeves was talking about, Matthews contented himself with saying that he was hardly in a position to tell. Apparently, that satisfied Reeves. "No, no, of course not," he agreed almost to himself. "I suppose that is *not* a matter that you would understand." Then, apparently unaware that he was not expressing himself with perfect courtesy he went on, "But then exactly what do you want? Clearly you have not digested everything in the letter — it is a very complex letter, I agree, and reflects an interesting personality — equally clearly you have no idea of quite why Miss Trent showed it to you. There I have even more sympathy with you, for who can wholly understand a woman? All the same I think — mind you, I only said that I think — unless she can give a very convincing explanation, it would probably be better that I had nothing more to do with her. After all, why should I expect her to rise to my heights?" For the moment he had apparently forgotten Matthews. Then he turned back to him suddenly and repeated the request to know exactly what it was that he wanted.

"I am concerned with asking you in what circumstances and especially at what time you posted that letter. As I want you to make a voluntary statement about it, it is only fair that I should tell you that I have not seen the letter myself, that I do not know when it was posted or where or what the point is. Inspector Hardwick knows all those points."

"Then why is he not here? Why should I be fobbed off with a subordinate?"

"Possibly he has more important things to do." For once Matthews' outward composure was slightly upset and he answered brusquely.

"More important things to do! And may I ask what in this case is more important than I?"

"You may ask anything you like but it would be more helpful if you answered the questions put to you. When did you post that letter?" Matthews felt his temper rising.

"How should I know? Do you remember where you post every letter that you send?"

"No. But this was an important letter. I want to be very careful not to put things into your mind—"

"You would find that difficult."

"Very likely. Nevertheless I believe that the danger of doing that is the reason for the Inspector's absence. But perhaps we might be able to think it out. *Where,* for instance, did you post it?"

"Oh! The post office just opposite our place. I remember that perfectly well." Reeves seemed mollified by the explanation of Hardwick's absence and therefore was ready to cooperate. "Really, you know," he went on; "I find this on second thoughts very interesting — very interesting indeed, and the point that strikes me as worthy of investigation is that I have no idea at all!"

"Surely! Try to think. It was a very important letter. And you are so sure of all your movements and so clear in your descriptions." It was a positive relief to Matthews to make so gross an exaggeration.

"Yes, quite, quite." Reeves accepted the flattery as the most natural thing in the world. "Let me think. I remember going down the steps of the office to post it. I was careful, I recollect, not to be seen. But why I cannot tell you. Then I came back again, again taking precautions. Yes, I think that that is right. I just went to the post office and I came back. I know that it was important that no one should see me — no one at all. I was very sleepy at the time." His mind seemed to be wandering as he spoke as if he were half in a trance.

Matthews allowed a silence to fall until the plain clothes man sitting clearly visible but unobtrusively at the side of the room had caught up with his shorthand. The scratching of his pencil reminded Matthews of the man's existence and he thought it only right to call attention to it. "You did this — you realise that I am having it taken down? — at what time? Before you went out to — lunch with Foster?"

"I hardly know," the voice was still dreamy. "It must, I suppose have been afterwards, because the letter described what happened. But I wrote it before. Because I knew exactly what was going to happen. I had rehearsed it all before. It was not a matter in which I could allow anything unforeseen to occur. I had to be absolutely right on all the details. Absolutely consistent. This letter though was not in the plan." His voice slid away and for a few seconds there was silence. Then he resumed again his ordinary manner. "What are you talking about? It was always part of my plan. In fact it *was* the second part of the plan. I was pretty sure you would go prying into things and a great deal of confusion to yourselves your prying will have caused I have no doubt."

"Then you wrote the letter before you went out to lunch?"

"Yes. Oh, yes. I am quite sure of that."

"And you posted it on your way out to lunch?"

"I thought you were not to put anything into my mind. I tell you I cannot remember. It was a wholly separate action, quite apart from going out to lunch. It was just something that I had to do, quietly, and without anyone knowing. What made it so difficult was that I was so sleepy."

"I see." Matthews was quite convinced that he did nothing of the sort, but it was no good telling Reeves that. He wondered very much whether he was getting what Hardwick wanted. Perhaps he had better try another line. "I know nothing about it and, as I said before, you must not think that I am suggesting anything to you, but it seems unusual—"

"But I am unusual. Do please realise that! You keep on forgetting it."

"I wonder if I do? However, shall we say 'unusual' even for so remarkable a man as yourself? To describe something before you did it and post a letter, even a confidential letter, about it before it happened. However well one plans things, circumstances have a habit of altering details."

"Exactly, Sergeant, exactly. You have probably found that out by now."

"Well, then — would it not be more..." he hesitated for a word. Neither "reasonable" nor "rational" were likely to be well received, "...probable that you wrote it after you came back from lunch and posted it then. You told us, you will remember, that after talking the matter over with Mr Shergold, you felt unexpectedly tired and had to rest for a few minutes. Could you not have written and posted it then?"

"Written it, no. There was certainly no time for that. Posted it? Well, perhaps that is possible. It would account for the feeling of tiredness that is associated in my mind with posting it. Also with the desire, which I remember now, of not letting Arthur know."

"Of not letting Mr Shergold know?"

"Yes. I felt that he did not want Cynthia brought into it. He had a — well, perhaps there is no need to mention the line that he took about Miss Trent."

"I see. To sum up then, you are sure that you wrote the letter earlier in the day—"

"Or the day before. I forget. Really, I am surprised that my mind is not clearer on this point. Most unusual with me to be so uncertain."

"As to posting it, you are not sure of the time, but you think it may have been after describing the events of the afternoon to Mr Shergold. You have given us also a description of your reaction and feelings at the time. Is that right?"

"Perfectly."

"Perhaps then we could simplify that and get it down on paper."

"Is that necessary?"

"I certainly cannot make you. If you would prefer not to sign anything, you need not do so. It is for you to decide. In view however of your previous detailed statement, I thought that perhaps—"

"You are right, Sergeant. Perfectly right. I am now as at all times quite prepared to assist you." Once more Reeves struck an attitude, but then had to end rather lamely. "The only trouble is that this time I am not absolutely sure of my facts."

Nor for that matter was Matthews. That the postmark gave a contradiction to what was being said was unknown to him too. "Nevertheless," Hardwick said when he came to read it later, "I am glad on the whole that I got you to ask him about that instead of doing it myself. Also that I kept you partly in ignorance. Anyone knowing of the time that that letter was posted would have been bound to have said too much. As it is, we have a most interesting exposition and not the least interesting part of it are the points which, for once, he is unaware are of interest to us. Everything else that he has said since he came here has been carefully prepared, rehearsed even, I think that it is fair to say; but here we have had several details of whose importance he is quite unaware." He actually beamed on Sergeant Matthews. "Though," as that conscientious person said to himself, "I must admit that I prefer being praised for what I have wittingly done." But anyhow he forgot entirely his original displeasure at being made to do the task and his acid remarks to Troughton.

* * *

TO MAKE A FURTHER EXAMINATION, Mr Pennington wrote — and Mr Pennington was glad to have the opportunity to write his report in peace. The absence of the Inspector was a positive relief to him and, his investigation largely finished, he ignored the passage of time and stayed on in the room that had once been devoted to those who were fire-watching. Mr Shergold, with a shrug of his shoulders, had left him with a parting shot that he was responsible for the safety of Company's books and papers. He was indifferent to that. He was indifferent even to food and drink and he had no idea how he would get home. Probably he would not. He might snatch a few hours on the divan bed so thoughtfully provided. He might — ah yes, there was an idea! — he might find out if the night-shift were on duty. Perhaps he could get hold of this man Yabsley. It would be helpful to have a talk with him. It would look well too in the report. But he was going to write that report that night.

Meanwhile he headed his sheet of foolscap "Shergold Engineering Company" and after underlining it neatly he went on:

I have visited the above-named Company in order to make a further examination of their books, papers and records and in particular to inquire into the following points:

1. The payment of wages, both before and after the introduction of a special check brought in by us after the discovery of certain frauds carried out by a firm in Liverpool on the Admiralty.

2. The sale of scrap.

3. Allegations made against the firm as to (a) improper charging up of labour to the Ministry (b) improper use of materials.

I regret to have to state that all of these subjects call for further investigation. The facts that I have already discovered lead me to believe that there have been irregularities under all these heads. It will not be possible for me fully at this juncture to substantiate all the points that I propose to raise but I have thought it my duty to submit this preliminary report in order that the Ministry may be informed of the position.

He stopped for a moment and picked up a folder. In the oblong at the top left-hand corner he wrote underneath the printed words "From Whom": *"Thomas Pennington, FCA."* Underneath "Date" he put *"April 20th—21st, 1945"* — he rather liked the touch that implied the burning of the midnight oil though it was perhaps conveyed too subtly for his superiors to notice it. But it was the heading "Subject" which had made him pick up the folder at that moment. *Preliminary report on alleged irregularities concerning the Shergold Engineering Company Ltd.* He wrote it neatly in three lines making a break after "irregularities" and before the Company's name which again he underlined. He had not wanted to forget to include the word "Preliminary" and for that purpose he had digressed. Then he continued his report.

Before a final report can be submitted, I shall require technical assistance, particularly as to the matters outlined in paragraphs (2) and (3).

The investigation has arisen on account of the death by violent means of *Mr Barry Foster, ACA, employed in this department. Mr Foster had been engaged in examining the costs of the company in question.*

He stopped for a minute and thought about it. It would, of course, he decided, be very wrong to say anything detrimental to Foster's character. At the same time to rush into a precipitate defence of him might merely call attention to the shortcomings of Foster — and of Pennington's own control of his branch, if there were any.

"Well," he said to himself, "if there are any, they will no doubt come out and there it is." He went on writing steadily.

> *The circumstances of Mr Foster's death are no doubt well known to the Department from statements in the press and call for no comment by me.*
>
> *Using the powers which the Ministry has acquired under Regulation 55 (1). of the Defence (General) Regulations 1939 and which they have delegated to me when necessary, I insisted on taking possession of all the books and records in the managing director's private safe. Part of these books had been, I infer, destroyed but enough remained to convince me that for certain periods in 1941 and 1942 two wage books were in use. One of these was used in the payment of the workmen which was carried out generally by the Managing* Director *but sometimes by the* Works Manager. *This book, which contained a truthful and accurate record of the wages paid, necessarily since it was seen by the Works* Manager, *could also be produced if called for by an official of the* Ministry *for checking and comparison with, for instance, insurance cards or if called for by any of the Technical branches of the Ministry who might compare it, for instance, with the number of men physically present.*
>
> *The second book contained the same details as the first but with the addition of, on an average, four extra names. The total in this book agrees with the weekly cheques drawn and is included in the financial*

accounts of the Company, the extra wages being charged to "Non-Productive Wages Account" i.e., to those wages not included direct. They were however included in overheads and were therefore charged indirectly to the Ministry and such other Government departments as are concerned.

The wages books are not complete, and I cannot therefore give an exact figure of the wages included under this heading but for two periods of fourteen and twenty-two weeks in 1940 and 1941 respectively I find the amounts, including Insurance, to be, £285.4.7. and £448.1.10.

It is possible that a defence will be raised that the persons so shown as paid were in fact employed but not in doing work of the type charged direct to contracts. They might for instance be storemen, yard labour, cleaners or other such persons. Such an explanation however would not call for two wage books nor for the fact that as the result of such discreet enquiries as I have permitted myself to make, no persons of the names of these extra men and women are known to anyone to whom I have spoken. Nor are persons of such names at present employed by the Company. It is a matter of uncertainty to me as to whether enquiries were ever raised by the Inland Revenue in connection with tax on such wages.

The Ministry is of course aware that after the discovery of the fraud on the Admiralty mentioned above, instructions were given for a periodical test examination of insurance cards. Mr Foster's reports of varying dates have mentioned that this test has been carried out. There are marks in the books which may be those made by him which would support his statements. If this is so, when the first check was carried out, he was given the shorter, i.e. correct, wages book for which, of course, all the cards are present. The total however would not agree with the financial books and it is regretted that Mr Foster cannot have traced the total into the cash book.

On the second occasion the longer book was produced but it would appear that false cards were produced to him. It is of course common knowledge that National Health Insurance Cards can be obtained on demand, but that Unemployment Insurance cannot. It is my belief that these were obtained, possibly by purchase, from men who were in distressed circumstances and who would then report that they had lost them. This matter can be taken up since the actual cards remain in the safe and thus permit of the men being traced. Of course had the cards been stamped in the ordinary and legitimate way of employment, they would not have remained in the safe as they would have been required by the individuals concerned. I also noticed that the names which I believe to be fictitious change at this date to those on the cards. It is my opinion that Mr Foster could not reasonably have discovered this fraud — if fraud it be proved to be.

In addition it is possible that Mr Foster expressed his intention of making some further check of a more exhaustive nature — possibly including "Pay As You Earn" cards, (though little real value would be obtained by an examination of these); it may have been so, or it may have been that whoever was responsible for the additional names heard some rumours to that effect. In any case the extra names disappear from the books at about the date of the introduction of 'Pay As You Earn' and after this date I have not found a second wages book.

In the Company's accounts the total wages fall by an approximate average of £20 (twenty pounds) a week. In view of the fact that this sum is not very large it is possible that whoever committed the fraud decided at this point that the trouble involved was too great for the result obtained.

The weekly total to the nearest pound of wages paid from 5.1.41 to 29.12.44 inclusive is given in Schedule 1.

Conclusion.

A) It is my opinion that a prima facie case of fraud is made out and should be answered. I shall however require the Department's instructions before proceeding further on these lines.

B) The exact amount of the fraud is not likely ever to be ascertained accurately. It amounts probably to about £20 a week for roughly two years, i.e. some £2,000.

C) It is my opinion that if a fraud was carried out, it was perpetrated by or with the knowledge of Mr Shergold the Managing Director. It seems possible, even probable, that he has placed the sums in question in his own pocket. It is my belief that Mr Reeves, at present detained for the alleged murder of Mr Foster, is not implicated since he returned from the Forces at a date subsequent to the cessation of the alleged frauds.

D) I have not considered it part of my duty to determine whether or not Mr Foster's death is in any way concerned with this alleged fraud.

Having completed a paragraph that, like its predecessor, was not without its moment of drama, Pennington quietly picked up a second sheet and headed it ("2. Scrap.") Before however he was prepared to report fully on that, he would rather like a few words with Yabsley. He was in no way acquainted with the works of the Shergold Engineering Company, but he decided to go in search of him. On the whole Mr Pennington was enjoying himself.

* * *

HARDWICK SAT READING Doctor Grantham's much overdue report.

So far as it dealt with the time or cause of death or afforded further evidence as to the by now famous lunch party, it added very little to what had been previously stated. As to time it was still the doctor's opinion that two o'clock was the most likely hour, but he was clearly very averse to being definite, let alone dogmatic, in the matter. The post mortem had shown no cause of death other than the strangling and Foster had not been, for instance, poisoned nor had he had heart disease, though his corpulence had been a tax on his heart, and this had probably contributed to the ineffectiveness of his resistance. The meal that he had had before had not been so heavy a one as Reeves' description would have led anyone taking it too literally to believe. There was no signs of *pâté maison*, but apparently it was unlikely that there would have been. On the other hand it was confirmed that venison was the chief course of the meal.

It was, however, when Doctor Grantham came to the details of the strangling and the bruising of Foster's throat that he became interesting. The bruises, he wrote, had been the cause of the delay in the rendering of the report. *I think therefore that I had better explain the matter in detail. I will try to put it in simple language.* Hardwick grunted and remarked to himself that he wished that these doctors would not assume that everyone except themselves was half-witted. Then he went on reading.

If strangulation is effected by the use of the normal hand, I should expect to find one bruise made by the thumb on the left of the larynx as you look at it and four to the right of the larynx made by the fingers. That is, of course, if the strangulation was carried out by the right hand. If the left hand were used, the position of the bruises would be reversed.

So far, I have been dealing with a man standing in front of the person strangled. If he stood behind we should get, as it were, a looking-glass effect and the sides would be reversed. It would be difficult to be sure if the bruises were those made by a right-handed man operating from in front or a left-handed man approaching his victim from behind. I think that very careful examination would enable me to do so, but in this case the exact circumstances do not arise since Foster was not strangled by a man using all the fingers of either hand.

I believe that you examined the body yourself. If so, you will probably have noticed that there was a fairly long and heavy bruise to the right of the larynx. To the left was a similar bruise but not quite so heavy while below, almost straight on the middle of his throat, but if anything slightly to the right were three lighter marks. These bruises could only have been caused by a right-handed man approaching Foster from the front and using the thumb and first finger of his right hand or by a left-handed man coming from behind and using the thumb and first finger of his left hand.

Hardwick put the report down for a minute. "Why," he said to Matthews, "does he assume that a right-handed man could not use his left hand and vice-versa?"

"Or he might be ambidextrous. But if you leave out the words 'right-handed man' and 'left-handed man' it doesn't alter the sense."

"Quite. Then why couldn't he do so. However—" Hardwick went back to the report. He found Doctor Grantham beginning to be technical.

I must explain, he wrote, *that the bones that work the hand are very complex. Broadly speaking they consist of the carpals or wrist bones, the metacarpals or bones of the palm of the hand, and the fingers. The fingers consist of three phalanges with a joint between each, the first phalanx extends from the knuckle to the first joint in the fingers, the second from the first joint to the second joint while the third phalanx consists of the tip of the finger beyond the second joint.*

Again Hardwick looked up to make sure that Matthews had reached the same point in his copy of the report. "You were right," he said. "He did have to go and look up his textbooks on anatomy."

Matthews grunted. "I should have thought he would have known that much without a textbook."

"You never can tell what people know and what they have to confirm. Why even we…" He went on reading.

The first problem which presented itself to me was to find a reason why anyone should use only the thumb and first finger and not the whole hand. The reason which would naturally occur to one was that we were dealing with a man who had lost the remaining three fingers of his hand. Such cases are all too common owing to war injuries.

Assuming such a case I had to consider the effect of amputation at varying points of the hand. Amputation on the third phalanx only is rare. It is unsightly and not very helpful. Very much the same applies to an operation which removes the second and third phalanges. Amputation to leave the first phalanx only is frequently carried out in cases where it is specially desired that, for some occupational reason, the first phalanx should be retained for the purpose of gripping some object, the tools with which a man works for instance. The most common amputation though is that which removes all the phalanges and leaves nothing beyond the knuckles.

Hardwick nodded. It was quite true. A man with stumps beyond the knuckles would look very odd and unsightly.

I came to the conclusion, Grantham's report went on, *that in the case with which we are concerned we could certainly omit all question of a natural use of a hand which had retained any of the second or third phalanges since in those cases the remains of the fingers must have caused bruises not very dissimilar to those of an ordinary hand and certainly further to the side of the larynx than was the case. Two cases then remained, that of a hand retaining the first phalanx of those three fingers and that of a hand having no phalanges.*

I next considered what would be the natural way to use a hand consisting, for the purpose, of only the thumb and the first finger. For myself I should have used it horizontally, as it were, so as to get the use of all that portion of the hand which is between the thumb and first finger. Quite clearly this would have produced a quite different series of bruises, one on each side of the larynx and some way from it. This method was clearly discarded by whoever killed Foster. He decided to use his hand in a vertical position.

In this position it is not easy to get the force required which it must be remembered even allowing for the possibility of Foster's heart having given way so that he could not put up a fight, had to be sufficient not only to cause death by strangulation but to overcome any initial resistance. I cannot be certain, but it is my opinion that it is more probable that strangulation was effected not from in front with the first finger and thumb of the right hand but from behind by the left hand reinforced by the right.

The position of the head, drawn backwards, and of the body, which was in a position to suggest that Foster had been attempting to rise from his chair, are both consistent with this opinion.

It is, however, quite certain that the murderer was not a left-handed man who had lost three fingers. He may, or may not, have been left-handed but he was in possession of all the fingers of the hand that strangled Foster on Wednesday, April 18th, at about two o'clock in the afternoon.

Doctor Grantham had enjoyed writing that sentence. There had been moments when he had felt that the police had not quite appreciated his work, had even been trying to hurry him and to express concern that they had not had his detailed conclusions earlier. Very well then. People were always in a hurry but at least they would now see that he had something to consider carefully and that a rushed opinion might have been wrong. He had no idea whether it would be important to the case, not having had the benefit of Reeves' acquaintance, but he not unnaturally suspected that it was. It might well, he could imagine, be quite sensational.

Then he had gone on to give his reasons.

I have reached the point when I must give my reasons for saying that no man who had used his whole hand, nor a man who had lost the second or second and third phalanges of his hand would produce the bruises which in fact were produced, if he used his hand naturally.

If the man had lost all his phalanges, he would have produced no bruise at all other than that caused by the finger and thumb remaining.

If the first phalange remained, which I at first thought was the state of affairs, he would have slight bruises of the type which I found, but these bruises would be to the left of the larynx as you look at it, that is to say on the same side as the fingers which remained.

If strangulation was carried out by someone who wished to simulate the effect of strangulation being effected by a man who had lost three fingers, he would have to clench his three fingers. If he clenched them normally the bruising would be straight down the centre of the trachea, that is to say straight down the middle line of the neck.

But if the man clenched his fingers excessively, the bruise would tend to be on the same side as that made by the thumb.

In the case of Foster the bruises answered to the last condition and it is therefore my opinion that death was caused by a man in full possession of all the fingers of his hand but who was anxious, for reasons not known to me, to pretend that he was not. In fact so anxious was he to produce this appearance that he doubled them back as far as he could — and the more he did so, the less realistic was his impersonation.

Had he been wise, he would have used the hand horizontally. This would have given a further series of problems and with which I need not worry you since they are purely theoretical. I think that they too would have been capable of a similar solution.

For reasons given above I think that the murderer stood behind his victim and used the right hand to help the left. Indeed this would be even more necessary as the ability to obtain sufficient pressure would be diminished by the artificial position of the hand.

Hardwick put the report down and thought a minute. "Fits like a glove," he said. "He will be awfully annoyed, but I shall have the greatest pleasure in releasing Mr Guy Reeves from detention. It's going to take a little proving, but I know quite well who done it. Don't you?"

"Oh yes," Matthews answered.

* * *

THE BARMAN at Oddenino's looked at a further selection of photographs. Over one he stopped and hesitated. "I should like to see him in person, but I think that's the chap." The waiter was more definite. "That's him," he said. "He won't get me to give him no lunch again."

Only at Cricklewood was the conductress less sure. "Keep on worrying a girl," she said. "Here, if I've got to pick one, I'll have this. Though it ain't no oil-painting."

The selection committee had been unanimous.

* * *

"INSPECTOR? Is it all right to ring you up so early?"

"Who is that? Oh! Mr Pennington. Yes, quite all right. In fact I don't really regard it—"

"Oh, don't you? I do. I'm generally much later but today — well, in fact I've been up all night." Mr Pennington though he might not have known it, was giving a realistic imitation of an ingenuously pleased school-boy. Hardwick could not help smiling as he replied, "And what have you been doing?"

"Working! It will look frightfully funny on my time sheet and I don't suppose anyone will believe me, but there it is. I have got nearly all the business about wages settled and I have virtually proved that the directors — or anyhow one of them — regarded the scrap as just his own 'perks,' if I may use the phrase, and kept the proceeds himself. That you know, Inspector, is not only a fraud on the Inland Revenue. It is a fraud on *us*."

Inspector Hardwick could not help it. "Go on!" he exclaimed.

"Fact, I assure you. And then finally I have seen this man Yabsley—"

"The devil you have. I am not quite sure that I intended you — In fact I thought he was not there."

"He came in for a bit anyhow last night. It was about him I wanted to talk to you, or rather about something that he told me. Inspector, could you...could you...? I don't want to say too much on the telephone. You never can be sure you know. But could you meet me at Victoria Station? It's not far off from — you know where I mean."

Hardwick smiled gravely. "Very well; I will meet you there."

"Under the clock? That will be delightful." If only Mr Pennington could get mixed up with a few more murders and half a dozen additional frauds, there was clearly a chance of his becoming quite young again. In quite a short while he was joined there by the Inspector and jubilantly proceeded to Elizabeth Street. It was, he explained, a matter primarily for the Ministry and if the Inspector did not mind, he would open the question himself. The Inspector did not mind, and Mr Pennington did open it. Moreover opened it to some considerable effect. In fact he dealt with Mr Benson by methods so rough that the Inspector would have hesitated to use them. It was too much altogether for that astute receiver of scrap and maker of oddments. He came clean, almost too clean, for like many of those who confess their sins, he took very good care to call attention to those of others. Apparently, it was all the fault of the wicked employer and his even more wicked staff, (Tommy Yabsley would have been quite surprised to know what a villain he was), but only a very little was it the fault of the much-tempted Mr Benson.

Whether really anything could be fastened on to Mr Benson, sufficient to justify proceedings against him, both Pennington and Hardwick really doubted, but Benson had no doubts. "So you see, gentlemen, when he came to me the other morning and told me to think it was a bit after one when it was about half-past twelve, I had to say 'yes'. But I didn't say it — be fair now, Inspector! I didn't, did I? I sort of was a bit doubtful like."

* * *

ARTHUR SHERGOLD RAISED HIS EYEBROWS. His fingers fidgeted with that component the absence of whose manufacture in any large quantity had been such a blow to his Company. "To what," he asked, "am I indebted the honour of this dual visit? The hours kept by Scotland Yard are unknown to me but to see an official of the Ministry working on a Saturday shocks me."

"I always do work then," Pennington answered simply. He was a sufficiently experienced civil servant to be perfectly used to the wild statements made by the general public and to be almost completely impervious to them.

"You may work on Saturdays — Sundays too for all I know," Shergold retorted, "but I do not believe that you usually visit contractors. In fact, I generally reckon that those two days are the only ones in which I may hope to be reasonably safe from Government interference."

"Quite right in general. But the circumstances here are unusual."

"Very. In fact that might almost be called an understatement. But they also make me very busy."

"No doubt. With the Inspector's leave, I will come straight to the point."

"Just a minute. I have an idea that you are going to make some allegations against my Company. Is that any business whatsoever of Inspector Hardwick's?"

"Any information about this Company is of interest to us at present."

"That is an evasive answer, Inspector."

"It's a perfectly true one and in any case, it is the only one that I propose to give."

"I see. I do not suppose — in these days — that it will have any effect, but I must emphatically protest at your presence."

"I will make a note of your protest." Hardwick answered gravely. "Now, Mr Pennington."

"I am afraid," Pennington started a little nervously but clearly with every intention of doing what he had to do, "that I have to ask you to give me an explanation of three matters connected with the way in which your Company has been run."

"And if I will not?"

"I shall have to report the matter to the Ministry and leave them to draw their own conclusions." Knowing perfectly well that his "Preliminary Report" was already on its way, Pennington blushed slightly. It was the first time in his life that he had ever got so near to telling a falsehood. "But," he went on, "I suggest that it would be better if you did give me your explanation. It is only fair to you to have an opportunity to state your side of the case. Possibly the earlier the better. It might save trouble. Besides, first impressions are hard to eradicate." Again Pennington blushed. He had already provided the Ministry with its first impression.

"Let me hear your points and I will then decide whether I shall answer them or not. It may be wiser to provide myself with legal advice — of a different kind to that with which you have provided yourself."

"That is quite fair. The first point is..." Pennington plunged into a detailed explanation of the false entries in the duplicated wages book. It sounded to Hardwick to be a very comprehensive and convincing statement, but apparently it produced very little effect on Shergold. He sat there, generally with his elbows on his desk, the tips of his fingers just touching. Occasionally he dropped a hand to toy with the rejected component that lay by his inkpot and pen tray. On his face was no expression whatever. "Does that," he asked, seeing that Pennington had paused, "finish what you have to say?"

"On that point, but only on that point."

"I see. 'On that point then, but only on that point'," he mimicked, "I elect to answer. Yes, there are irregularities in the wages book. Yes, sums were charged to you which should not have been. Have you any proof that they were paid to me?"

"The wages book was under your control and yours only. Also the cash."

"Supposing that I paid them to someone else?"

"It would not seem to be very different from our point of view to your paying them to yourself. If that is your answer, who did you pay them to?"

"To Mr Foster. To an official of the Ministry very laxly supervised, whose good opinion was therefore important to us and who was given far too much discretion. You say that you paid. That is true, but if you employ second class people, pay them inadequately and let them both do and say what they like, you must expect to pay either directly or, to use your own phraseology, by 'allowing us to recover the expense in the overheads.'"

"I see. I note what you say, and I will duly include that in my report."

Inspector Hardwick looked at the rather shy man with renewed respect. He was certainly taking the accusation of lax supervision, which might be awkward for him, with remarkable calmness. The repercussion, whatever it might be so far as his own career was concerned, was not going to enter into his calculations. But fortunately Hardwick could do more than admire. He was able to help. "I should like," he said, "to mention something which is within my own knowledge only. I have read through the papers on which Mr Foster was working at the time of his death and it will save trouble if I agree at once that they contained nothing of interest on this subject. On the other hand I have also searched his flat and I have found some other notes. I will hand them to you later, Mr Pennington, and I think that they will convince you that Mr Foster was a better accountant than you imagined. He seems, shall we say, to have had his suspicions? Until I heard you just now, I hardly realised their significance. Moreover those suspicions had not been specifically aroused by you or your department."

"Really? I am rather glad of that — especially for Foster's sake. I shall certainly of course attach the notes of which you speak to my report. It can hardly do Foster any good now, but still..."

"Trust the Ministry to hang together!" Shergold broke in. "But may we return to so humble a person as myself? I have answered your first point. May we have the other two?"

"The second concerns the sale of scrap—"

"An infinitesimal point. I believe that I have failed to put through some small credit note."

"The third concerns the occupation of the night-shift. One of your employees called Yabsley—"

"A dirty tyke whom we have had to dismiss for drunkenness."

"—has made a statement, first of all to Miss Trent."

"I knew that that blasted little bitch would be in it somewhere. I propose to have her up at once and give her the sack." He pressed a bell on his desk three times. "That should bring her. That is if she has condescended to turn up this morning. She appears to have pleased herself in the last few days — Oh! that's where she went on Thursday. Whining round to you. My God!"

"You must please yourself as to her presence." Pennington went on unmoved. "I would however also inform you that the Inspector and I took a statement this morning from a man called Benson."

"Benson! I wish you and the Inspector would learn to mind your own business."

"There I entirely agree with you." The door was flung open to show Guy Reeves standing in it, with Cynthia nervously hovering in the background. "I have just," he said, "suffered the indignity of being released by your incompetent and ill-informed sergeant. I have been told that he does not believe a word that I say and when I asked where you are, Inspector, I was told that you are in my office, discussing my affairs without my consent and without my knowledge."

"Just a minute now. Are they your affairs?" Shergold broke in. "Judging by the amount of work that you have done this last year, I should say that it was *my* office and *my* company. After your performance of the last day or two, I shall have no difficulty in persuading our remaining shareholders that you are of no use to us. I shall buy your shares at a valuation — a fair valuation of about a halfpenny a hundred shares."

"And if that is what you have reduced their value to, have you got the impertinence to sit there and tell the world of the muddle you have made?"

"My muddle! Your incompetent neglect you mean."

"Neglect! After what I did for you on Wednesday, do you dare say that? Even if this half-witted Inspector does refuse to believe what I have told him clearly, you at least know that I did do it. You will be telling me next that you did it yourself. You are always trying to take the credit for everything."

"As a matter of fact," Hardwick began slowly, but Reeves interrupted him before he could go any further. "A precious lot you know about facts. I come to you and I tell you a wholly coherent and connected story—"

"Having carefully arranged some flaws in it and seen that those flaws should come to my notice."

Reeves stopped suddenly and looked in a surprised and rather dazed way at Hardwick. Then he brought a chair up to

Shergold's desk. He appeared ill at ease and his hand gripped and ungripped the steel component with its heavy machined head. Then his face seemed to clear. "So," he began slowly, "it was the irregularities that convinced you — it was what I did that convinced you — it was I who proved to you that I had not — only I had. By George, I have been clever after all." He leant back, satisfied. Then his hesitation seemed to come back to him. "Inspector, I — I did do it, didn't I?"

"No, sir. Not one jot or tittle of it. However much it may annoy you, it is my duty to inform you that you are wholly and completely innocent of the murder of Barry Foster. In fact I think that Sergeant Matthews has already told you—"

Reeves recovered his poise. "Nonsense. I told you all about the lunch—"

"Which you never had. You had two rum cocktails on Wednesday, but you had no lunch at all that day."

"Didn't I? I do remember that I felt very hungry all day. Where did I have those cocktails anyhow?"

"Next door. In the fire-watcher's room. They were quite strong cocktails and they also contained a certain amount of the sedative Codeine Compositum. You slept very well after it though there still remained beating in your mind the lesson that you have been so carefully taught. You went to sleep about twelve o'clock but, drugged though you were, you had had impressed on you so carefully that you were to do something that you half woke up. You knew that you had to go out without being observed, do something; and come back equally unobserved and so you got up and you posted a letter."

"The one to me?"

"The one to you, Miss Trent, which you rightly showed to me."

"I don't think she was right to show you my letter at all."

"Shall we leave that point alone? And don't sniff, please, Miss Trent. You woke up again, Mr Reeves, I imagine about three o'clock and again you talked over the already carefully rehearsed story. It would puzzle you, as it puzzled me, to know when your rehearsals were before and when they were after the, shall we say, main performance. I fancy though that now and then you were wilful and insisted on awkward details — in one case something that was very much more than a detail — and in others you varied an incident after the event. Thus for instance an unfortunate subordinate of mine called Troughton has spent some time looking for confirmation of an alleged and wholly imaginary taxi ride. Not that it matters. Oh, but by the way I am unable to prevent Constable Troughton from pursuing other and wilder goose chases today. You will have to apologise, Mr Pennington, to your friend and his cricketing son for any inconvenience to which they may have been put."

"What on earth has all this got to do with the matter in hand?" Shergold broke in. "Do stop fidgeting with that thing, Guy."

"I shall do just what I like with it. Are you suggesting, Inspector, that I could not get a taxi when I wanted one?"

"I am suggesting that you did not need one."

"You will be telling me next that Foster is not dead."

"No. That I cannot do."

"Very well, then. You see you are wrong. I must have done it. What other story have you got to offer?"

"I have told you. That you rehearsed the matter with someone very clever and capable at suggesting things to you, of impressing them so firmly that you believed them to be true. You must excuse my saying that it *is* possible to induce you to dramatise yourself to that extent."

"Rubbish, Inspector. I keep a perfectly clear head and I know perfectly well what I have done — and what I am going to do."

"More especially what you are going to do. Only you do not always do it."

Unable to restrain his curiosity and seeing that Reeves' anger was getting too much for him, Pennington put in, "And what happened instead?"

"That while Mr Reeves slept, someone else made his way to Oddenino's, a little put out by a confusion made between that restaurant and the Café Royal, a confusion made partly on purpose perhaps. There he met a man whose investigations were at last reaching culminating point. The results were not, he believed, as yet put on paper, but if they were, they would be unpleasant for him. They must therefore be stopped finally and irrevocably. Hence the carefully prepared arrangements, beginning with the lunch. There was a difficulty there because the menu was not the same, naturally, at Oddenino's, as it would have been at the Café Royal, though his luck was in on the subject of venison. Moreover he had already had to drink two rum cocktails, to keep you company, Mr Reeves, and he found an additional two more than his temperate habits would stand. On the way, I should have said, he established an alibi, as he hoped, in Elizabeth Street, but that alibi has now broken down, along with a confession of other matters more of interest to Mr Pennington than to me."

"I must congratulate you both on your imagination," Shergold drawled, "but do not let it be imagined that my silence is giving consent to all these — pretty pictures."

"Not so very pretty," Hardwick commented. "But to resume. The meeting at Oddenino's was not when you said it was, Mr Reeves. It was at twelve forty-five, two cocktails quickly drunk took five minutes, lunch was served in forty minutes and two people left, one of them, who was in a hurry, leaving an insufficiently tipped and angry waiter behind. Buses run fast in these days and the 1.32 bus from Piccadilly Circus got them to Maida Vale by 1.50, including a slight comedy on the bus that should have been excluded. The party reached Foster's flat at 1.55 and there the murderer made his first and greatest mistake. He shut the window."

"And left a print on the handle? But I wore gloves." Reeves seemed to think that he had scored a point.

"Yes, you intended to, and your imitator did. But why should you? Why did you take such care to hide what you wanted to publish abroad? Namely your own presence there?"

"I wanted to do it my own way."

"Quite. But would *you* have shut the window?"

"N-no. That would hardly be like me."

"It would not. I understand that you have a reputation for being a fresh air fiend, whereas — Anyhow at two o'clock — not three — Foster was dead, with the bruises on his throat not being quite where they would have been had they been inflicted by your left hand. At two forty-five you were talking to the murderer; rehearsing carefully what you were supposed to have done and never had. It took longer than you thought. You were still under the influence of that vegamin from the Codeine Co and you may remember that you had to lie down afterwards for a bit longer still. Your time programme was again put out, but you left here all right at quarter-past four to come round to us."

"And how on earth can you prove all this?" Shergold asked, contemptuous to outward appearances at least. "You have done nothing to disprove what Reeves has told you."

"Oh yes, I have. There is first of all the letter. There is the medical evidence that the strangling was done not by a man who had lost the fingers of his left hand but by one who tried to simulate that and who over-acted. Finally there is the evidence of identification of several persons at Oddenino's and of a bus-conductress. It is my duty to arrest—" Suddenly the Inspector jumped up and seized his hands. "I know there is poison in that drawer, but you are not going to get at it. Matthews!" There was a slight confusion in the passage caused by Cynthia Trent unintentionally getting in the way.

"You did it — and tricked me!" Reeves was on his feet blazing with anger. The rejected component was between the finger and thumb of his over-developed left hand and suddenly he brought it down with all the force of which he was capable on Shergold's head. "You deprive me of my murder — as well as my money, my business and my reputation. So there you are, Inspector. You can take the change out of that! I wonder if anyone has ever got Scotland Yard to hold both hands before while they — hit. And hit successfully!"

The last words came slowly and emphatically, after a pause, through almost closed lips. Hardwick and Matthews were ruefully silent. Unexpectedly it was Pennington who spoke and even more unexpectedly he was distinctly angry. "Do *not* cry, Miss Trent," he shouted. "It's so—," his well-trained mind sought for the correct adjective, "it's so *inadequate*."

THE END

MURDER ISN'T EASY

CHAPTER ONE

There is a limit to the extent to which the folly of any man can be allowed to ruin a business, and beyond that limit Paul Spencer has certainly gone.

But first I suppose I must explain what our business is, because its very nature makes it peculiarly easy for one man, by pure incompetence and obstinacy, by an absolute refusal to listen to reason, to render entirely useless everything that is done by his colleagues, however well *they* may work.

Ours is not an old established business, nor is it commonly classed as one of the learned professions. Nevertheless, for the promotion of trade, nothing is more important. We are in fact Advertising Agents—a profession which many people are apt to look down upon. They fall into the common error of thinking that it is clever to sneer at an advertisement; they consider that the proper thing to do is to laugh at them, and they hint that they themselves could write very much better ones.

I only wish they would try before they make that sort of statement! They would soon find out that it is not just a trick of style, a parrot-like reproduction of stereotyped phrases, but literary work requiring the most careful thought. Why, in writing an advertisement every comma is important!—and can you say that of a novel?

Then think of the artistic side of it. Not only have your words to be illustrated—and it is the production department of the agency that produces the idea, though perhaps you may hire someone to do the actual mechanical process of drawing it; in fact we have a man called Thomas permanently employed to do lettering and what we call lay-outs—but you have to consider the kind of type you will use, and the size of the type, to weigh up the pros and cons of which word shall receive the maximum emphasis, of exactly what arrangements and spacing of the words will be most certain to attract the eye of the public, carry conviction, and produce action. Not an easy matter I assure you.

But before I go on to demonstrate why Paul Spencer must be got rid of, perhaps I had better say something of the history and organisation of NeO-aD (NeO-aD NeVeR NoDs is our slogan). It was originally my idea. I had studied advertising for a long while and I saw just where all the other agencies were wrong. They failed to study the sales problem of the client; their methods were not sufficiently modern, not thoroughly scientific. I had thought, of course, of attaching myself to one of the existing organisations and by exercising my personality, gradually grafting competency on to it, but so far as I could see, in all of them there would be too much deadweight to shift. So I decided to start my own company.

That very word "company" was the cause of my first mistake. I thought that it was necessary for a company to have capital, and that was a thing I had not got. Moreover, I thought that there was a great deal to be done by the secretary of a company, and so I got hold of Barraclough. Of course now I know that capital is really quite unnecessary. You just create some shares and some goodwill to go on the other side of the balance sheet and on you go. You can always borrow money somehow—besides one should never let oneself be kept down by want of cash. As for Barraclough's duties as secretary of the company, so far as I can make out he fills in one return a year for Somerset House. And for that I have saddled myself with having to give away a third of the profits that I earn!

Of course, as he is a director of NeO-aD, we do make Barraclough do something. He keeps the accounts for instance and arranges the contracts with the newspapers, what we call "space-buying", and looks after the general running of the office. Still we could have hired a clerk at two pounds a week to do that.

Barraclough, then, was my first mistake. My second was Paul Spencer. However well I might be able to design an advertising campaign, there had to be a client for whom to design it. I wanted therefore someone to go and find business. Someone who would get himself known, or rather who could get my work known, who could make people listen to him, in short who was a good salesman of the idea that NeO-aD should be appointed the agents of reputable companies.

After that all he would have to do would be to get their consent to the plans we proposed and keep in touch with them and keep them happy—take the directors and sales-managers out to lunch occasionally and so on—work which would take time that I should not be able to spare from my productive duties, but which surely was easy for an energetic, blustering type of man with plenty of personality and, of course, a reasonable amount of tact.

I must admit that Spencer seemed exactly the kind of man for whom I was looking.

I had known him for some time. He was a good-looking man of a fair type, rather fat perhaps, but that gave him an appearance (entirely erroneous as a matter of fact) of being good-tempered. He seemed to have plenty of life, plenty of bustle. He was, I knew, a little—how shall I put it?—coarse. He would never take 'No' for an answer, I was aware, but on the whole that seemed to me to be an advantage rather than the reverse. When once he saw a chance of getting the handling of a campaign into the office, I thought that he would never rest until the order was booked. Strange how when thinking of Spencer one falls into the jargon of salesmanship!

Up to a point I was right. I must admit that he is energetic, that he quite frequently brings in work. But what I had not realised was his incredible tactlessness. He *cannot* keep a client. Sooner or later he always goes and quarrels with him—generally sooner. Nor is he in the least persuasive. I supply him with ideas which any client must immediately accept if they were put to him in the right way, and he comes back not only without having convinced the man, but actually leaving him disgruntled. I have even known Spencer bring back alternative suggestions! And that brings me to another trouble I have with him.

I thought when we started that our respective spheres were clearly defined. Spencer was to keep his eyes open and find work. I was to do the work, and Barraclough was to make himself useful where he could—I am almost tempted to say, if he could. But I never expected to find Spencer making suggestions as to how a campaign should be prepared, any more than I thought that it would be necessary for me to do the contact work of the agency. Yet from the very first that is exactly what he did. To begin with I listened patiently enough to the amazing nonsense he talked, but after a while this began to pall. Besides one can point out the error in something which is nearly but not quite right, but it is impossible to argue about something which is merely fantastic. I began to find it harder and harder to counter his amateur suggestions for a selling plan, for, remember, he was always very able when it came to an argument. He never really had a case at all, but he always knew how to put it. Nothing would ever convince him that he would do very much better to mind his own business.

"My dear Latimer," he said to me the very first time I suggested it to him, "but it *is* my business."

As I write I can still remember vividly the confident tone of his voice. He was, of course, trying to make me lose my temper, that was one of his tricks, and he was very well aware that I hated sentences beginning 'My dear Latimer'. Besides, he generally used to call me Nicholas in those days; he only used my surname when he wanted to annoy me. However, I was determined to keep calm, and so instead of the direct negative which was the only real answer to the statement, I asked him in what way he thought it was his business.

"Your share, you know," I went on, "was, I thought, confined to getting work to do—just that, no more, except taking a third of the profits."

I could see that last remark had stung him. He must have known even then that he was not worth to the company what he took out of it.

He flushed a bit, but a little thing like that would not stop Spencer arguing. He even followed up my point, pretending to misunderstand it.

"Precisely, and I want to see that third as large as possible. Consequently it is very much my business to see that when I go to the Flaik-Foam people" (the campaign in question) "I have got something to show them which they are likely to take."

"I entirely agree. But what I am trying to suggest—I am afraid I cannot have put it clearly enough—is that it is my business to produce work which they will take; yours merely to go and show it to them."

"And you think with that I have only to go in order to conquer?"

I shrugged my shoulders. There was no need to put it so crudely as that! But that was Paul all over; always trying to put one in the wrong! It was unnecessary to imply that I was conceited. Besides, it was not true.

Seeing that he had hurt my feelings, Spencer shifted his ground cleverly.

"Let me try to explain on your own lines. You always tell me—and I quite see your point—that you cannot produce good work unless you are convinced of the merits of the product. You're always preaching 'conviction' to me. Fairly enough, I own. Well, I'm the same. I can no more go and sell that caption 'One Flaik-Foam Makes the Bath a Joy' to old Macnair than fly. It's too long and it's got too many capitals. You see, *I* am not convinced. Sorry," he added carelessly, in a voice that expressed no sorrow at all, "but there it is."

I think it is very greatly to my credit that I refrained from striking him there and then. And what was the result of all this obstruction? An absolute impasse! He, if you please, refused categorically to go down to the Flaik-Foam people with what he was pleased to describe as second-class work and I, naturally enough, refused to draw up another campaign to be the butt of his ignorant criticisms until he had at least attempted to sell that one.

Of course it would have been taken. I had recommended the use of various of the women's papers—*Woman and Beauty, Wife and Home* and *Woman's Journal* if I remember right. Besides which there was a rather daring suggestion of the *Royal* and one or two other magazines; and the copy was some of the most arresting I had ever written. Barraclough had added a few figures and some rather good notes about circulation. He did that sort of thing quite well at times.

But as Spencer refused to take it along to Macnair there seemed no chance of its ever being seen. After a fortnight I hit on the bright idea of sending it all by post and explaining that Mr. Spencer very much regretted that he had been unable to bring it down himself as he had been in bed with a cold.

When it was returned without comment I was very surprised until I learnt that Spencer had been down the day before my campaign reached them and explained that I had done some work, but that as I (if you please) was not satisfied with what had been produced, he must ask Macnair to wait another week. Of course Macnair had said that Flaik-Foam must be put on the market at once and he could wait no longer.

I often see the Flaik-Foam advertisements. They take quite a lot of space in the daily papers—*Sketch* and *Mirror* chiefly. Not a bad alternative to the women's papers, but the 'copy' strikes me as very poor. If only Spencer had been more sensible they might be using our copy instead.

WANT ANOTHER PERFECT MYSTERY?

GET YOUR NEXT CLASSIC CRIME STORY FOR FREE...

Sign up to our Crime Classics newsletter where you can discover new Golden Age crime, receive exclusive content and never-before published short stories, all for free.

From the beloved greats of the Golden Age to the forgotten gems, best-kept-secrets, and brand new discoveries, we're devoted to classic crime.

If you sign up today, you'll get:

1. A free novel from our Classic Crime collection.
2. Exclusive insights into classic novels and their authors and the chance to get copies in advance of publication, and
3. The chance to win exclusive prizes in regular competitions.

Interested? It takes less than a minute to sign up. You can get your novel and your first newsletter by signing up on our website www.crimeclassics.co.uk

facebook.com/crimeclassics
twitter.com/crimeclassics

Printed by Amazon Italia Logistica S.r.l.
Torrazza Piemonte (TO), Italy